George Brown, CLASS CLOWN

Let the Burping Begin

by Nancy Krulik

illustrated by Aaron Blecha

Grosset & Dunlap
An Imprint of Penguin Group (USA) Inc.

GROSSET & DUNLAP
Published by the Penguin Group
Penguin Group (USA) Inc., 375 Hudson Street,
New York, New York 10014, USA
Penguin Group (Canada), 90 Eglinton Avenue East, Suite 700,
Toronto, Ontario M4P 2Y3, Canada
(a division of Pearson Penguin Canada Inc.)
Penguin Books Ltd., 80 Strand, London WC2R 0RL, England
Penguin Group Ireland, 25 St. Stephen's Green, Dublin 2, Ireland
(a division of Penguin Books Ltd.)
Penguin Group (Australia), 250 Camberwell Road,
Camberwell, Victoria 3124, Australia
(a division of Pearson Australia Group Pty. Ltd.)
Penguin Books India Pvt. Ltd., 11 Community Centre,
Panchsheel Park, New Delhi—110 017, India
Penguin Group (NZ), 67 Apollo Drive,
Rosedale, Auckland 0632, New Zealand
(a division of Pearson New Zealand Ltd.)
Penguin Books (South Africa) (Pty.) Ltd., 24 Sturdee Avenue,
Rosebank, Johannesburg 2196, South Africa

Penguin Books Ltd., Registered Offices:
80 Strand, London WC2R 0RL, England

Text copyright © 2010 by Nancy Krulik.
Illustrations copyright © 2010 by Aaron Blecha.
All rights reserved. The books in this bind-up were originally published in 2010 by
Grosset & Dunlap as *Super Burp!*, *Trouble Magnet*, and *World's Worst Wedgie*.
This edition published in 2012 by Grosset & Dunlap, a division of
Penguin Young Readers Group, 345 Hudson Street, New York, New York 10014.
GROSSET & DUNLAP is a trademark of Penguin Group (USA) Inc. Printed in the U.S.A.

The Library of Congress has catalogued the individual books
under the following Control Numbers: 2009036675 (#1 *Super Burp!*),
2009042078 (#2 *Trouble Magnet*), 2010003991 (#3 *World's Worst Wedgie*)

ISBN 978-0-448-46284-4   10 9 8 7 6 5 4 3 2

For Jeffrey, who has done his share
of burping over the years.–NK

For Nicky again and always–my Burpin' Bride–AB

George Brown, CLASS CLOWN

Super Burp!

by Nancy Krulik

illustrated by Aaron Blecha

Grosset & Dunlap
An Imprint of Penguin Group (USA) Inc.

Chapter 1

Yo George,
never thought I'd say this, but I think it stinks that you won't be going to our school anymore. Now I'll be the only one in class 4A telling jokes, and my jokes always sounded better next to yours.

At least at your new school, you can be the funny guy.

Your pal,

Kadeem

George lay on his bed and stared at Kadeem's page in the **Good-bye, George** book the kids at his old school had made

for him. All the fourth-graders had written something. But Kadeem's page was the one that made George the saddest and the maddest. Sad because now he had no friends to tell jokes to. And mad because **Kadeem made it sound like his jokes were funnier than George's**. And that wasn't true. **No way!**

George reread what Kevin, his best friend, had written. At least Kevin used to be George's best friend. **Could you stay best friends with someone far away?**

George,
I was just thinking about the time in third grade when you put the fake spider on Mrs. Darkman's chair in the cafeteria. I never heard anyone scream so loud. I laughed so hard, milk came out of my nose.

Boy, will I miss you,
Kevin

P.S. Here's a photo so you don't forget what I look like.

George started to laugh. No one was more afraid of bugs than mean **Mrs. Jerkman**. (That was what George had always called his strict third-grade teacher—at least behind her back.) Freaking her out was always fun.

George turned the page in his book. The next note was from Suzanne Lock.

George,

Good-bye.
Suzanne

Even seeing that cheered George up. Suzanne hadn't wanted to write anything. Her teacher had made her do it. Not that George blamed Suzanne. It wasn't like they'd ever been friends or anything.

But the note on the page next to Suzanne's was from one of George's really good friends.

Dear George,
I'm really going to miss you. You made me laugh—a lot. I think you are really brave. I'd be scared to move to a new town. But you don't seem scared at all. I know you will have a lot of friends in Beaver Brook.
    Your friend,
    Katie Kazoo
    PS—Thanks for the way-cool
nickname.

George thought Katie's last name, Carew, sounded like a kazoo. And **the nickname had stuck**.

Katie was a really good friend. And she was pretty smart. But she was wrong about George. He was scared to be living in a new town and starting in a new school today.

George had a lot of practice being the new kid. His dad was in the army and his family moved around a lot. But it was never easy. After spending two whole years in Cherrydale, he had almost started feeling like an "old" kid. Then—*BAM*—**here he was in Beaver Brook**.

"George! It's 0-800 hours. Gotta get a move on! Front and center!"

His dad's deep voice echoed through the halls of their new house. It was a lot bigger than their old house. Even with all their furniture, it felt empty. In fact, the

long upstairs hallway would be great for skateboarding—**except his mom never let him skateboard in the house**.

George grabbed his backpack and headed downstairs. For a second, he thought about sliding down the banister. Then he stopped himself. That was something **the old George** would do. Now, besides being the new kid, he wanted to be a new George. And the new George didn't do dumb stuff like that, dumb stuff that got him into trouble.

The last time George slid down a banister was at his old school. He'd flipped over the side of the staircase and wound up with a black eye and a bloody nose. And not just a regular bloody nose. **A super-colossal bloody nose.** The kind that turns your nose into a blood fountain. The school nurse said she'd never seen anything like it. It had been sort of gross. But sort of cool, too.

"Got everything, honey?" George's mom asked as he reached the bottom of the stairs. "Pencils? Notebooks? Lunch?"

"Check, check, and check," George said.

"That shirt looks really nice," his mother told him.

"Thanks," George said. His new green T-shirt had a picture of a blob on the middle of it. It was really cool. **The perfect first day of school shirt.**

"Okay, soldier," his dad said. "Ready to march?"

"Yes, sir," George answered. He saluted his dad. His dad saluted back and then gave him a big bear hug.

"Then let's go," George's dad said.

As George headed to his new school, he thought about Cherrydale Elementary School. Not to brag, but everybody there liked him. He was famous for being the funny kid—the class clown. Of course, pranks also got him into more trouble than anyone. It seemed to George that he'd spent as much time in the principal's office as he had in class.

But that wasn't going to happen in Beaver Brook. **No more class clown!** George was turning over a new leaf. He was through with getting in trouble. He was going to act differently from now on. So differently, in fact, that **he'd decided to start school with a new last name**. His dad's last name was Brennan. And that was the last name George had used all his life. There was nothing wrong with that name. But from now on, George was using his mom's last name— Brown. **New name, new George.**

"George Brown," George murmured

quietly under his breath. "George Brown."

"What did you say?" his dad asked him.

"I was just trying out my new name," George explained.

"Oh," George's dad replied.

"You're okay about this, aren't you, Dad?" George asked his father.

"Sure." Only his dad didn't sound so sure. "I guess it'll just take a little getting used to. But I **understand wanting to change things up**. Look at me. I've traveled all over with the army. New people, new places. Lots of changes."

That was true. His dad's job was the reason the family was always moving. It was why George always seemed to be the new kid.

"But we're going to stay at this base for a while," George's dad continued. "At least I hope so. Your mom is really excited about opening her own store. I don't think she wants to pack up and move again."

"Yeah, I guess," George said. Having a dad in the army was cool. But having a mom who owned the Knit Wit—a shop that sold yarn, knitting needles, and beads—was, well . . . not so much.

George kept up with his dad's long strides, trying to ignore the nervous feeling in his stomach. His mom called it having **butterflies in your belly**. But that wasn't what it felt like. It was more like worms. **Big, long, slimy worms slithering around inside.**

They turned a corner. There it was. George stopped and stared at his new school. It was a redbrick building with a flagpole in front. Over the door it said **Edith B. Sugarman Elementary School**. Except for the name, it looked pretty much like all the other schools George had gone to.

"Edith B. Sugarman?" George
wondered. "Is that somebody famous?"

His dad shrugged. "Never heard of her.
But the name doesn't really matter. Your

new school has a fine reputation."

George didn't agree at all. **Names did matter.** A lot. And no one knew that better than George Brown.

Chapter 2

"Class, this is George Brown. George, we want to welcome you to class 401."

George stood there, looking at all the strange, new kids, while his teacher, Mrs. Kelly, introduced him. It was awful. The kids were all staring at him like he was a freak—**a two-headed ape** or something.

For a second, George considered tucking his hands under his armpits, and saying "Ook, ook, ook" like an ape.

Nobody did a better ape imitation than George.

But no. He was the new and improved George now. **There would be no ooking at school!**

"Who will volunteer to be George's buddy today?" Mrs. Kelly asked.

Right away, kids slid down in their seats, so Mrs. Kelly wouldn't pick them.

George wasn't surprised. No one ever wanted to be the new kid's buddy.

Finally, a girl with a long ponytail, who was wearing a yellow and green Little League jersey, raised her hand.

George was glad someone had finally volunteered. **He just kind of wished it hadn't been a girl.**

Mrs. Kelly nodded. "Thank you,

Julianna," she said. Then she smiled and turned to George. "Why don't you sit at the empty desk in the third row?"

George walked to his assigned seat. He hated assigned seats. What if he didn't like the kids on either side of him? What if he became best friends with that short kid with curly hair and the mouth full of braces who was sitting in the fourth row? Or what if he got to be friends with the kid in the blue shirt in the second row? He was wearing the kind of sneakers that turned into skates when you popped the wheels out. **A kid with shoes like that had to be cool.**

Of course, that wasn't a problem right now—George didn't have any friends. **The new kid never did.**

"Okay, class, take out your science notebooks," Mrs. Kelly said. Then she turned to George. "Yesterday we were talking about the first moon landing."

George smiled for the first time that day. **The moon landing.** They'd already studied that back in his old school.

George's old fourth-grade teacher, Mr. Guthrie, had made learning about space really awesome. He dressed like an astronaut and made the classroom look like NASA's Mission Control Center.

Mrs. Kelly wore her glasses on a chain around her neck and had a piece of tissue tucked in her sleeve. And the only decorations on the classroom walls were a poster that said READ and a chart showing how all the letters of the alphabet looked in cursive.

"Now, who can tell me the name of the first man to step foot on the moon?" Mrs. Kelly asked.

Two hands shot up. One hand was George's. The other hand belonged to the kid with the cool sneakers.

Mrs. Kelly pointed to George.

"Neil Armstrong," he told her.

"Yes!" Mrs. Kelly said. **"Very good, George."** Mrs. Kelly smiled—the kind of smile where her gums showed.

George smiled back. Already he was being **the new, improved, raise-your-hand George**.

"The second man to walk on the moon was Buzz Aldrin," the kid with the cool sneakers called out.

Instead of telling him that he wasn't supposed to call out without raising his hand, Mrs. Kelly said, "That's right, Louie. Thank you for sharing such an interesting fact."

One of the other boys in the class said, **"What kind of name is Buzz?"**

George knew that Buzz was just the astronaut's nickname. He even knew that the guy's real name was Edwin. But he kept quiet. Yes, he wanted to be the new, improved, paying attention George. But no, he didn't want to show off or make the other kids think he was a **brainiac geek** or anything.

Instead, he kept quiet and copied down everything Mrs. Kelly said or wrote on the blackboard. **There sure were a lot of**

notes. After a while, George had written so much that he felt like his hand was going to fall off. He could almost picture his hand breaking away from his wrist, and then walking across the floor—like something out of a **horror movie**.

Finally, Mrs. Kelly put down her chalk.

"Okay, everyone, let's get ready for gym," she told the kids. "Mr. Trainer is absent today. So I'm taking over your class. And we're going to do something really fun." Again **Mrs. Kelly smiled her big, gummy smile**.

As the kids lined up, George thought that he was ready for some fun.

The short boy with curly hair and braces walked down the hall next to George. "**I guarantee this is not going to be fun**," he said in a low voice. "So you can stop smiling."

"Why? What's she gonna make us do?" George asked nervously.

"You'll see," the boy answered. "But trust me. **It's the worst**."

Chapter 3

George followed his new classmates into the school gym. The kids all had sickly looks on their faces. But Mrs. Kelly looked really excited.

"Okay, everyone choose your partners," Mrs. Kelly said.

George frowned. **No one ever picked the new kid as a partner.** He was going to have to do whatever the awful thing was all by himself.

"I'll be your partner," the girl named Julianna said to George. "Since I'm your buddy, it's kind of my job."

George looked around the room. Was this the kind of thing you did with a girl?

Or was it the kind of thing fourth-grade guys did together?

Then he saw everyone else had broken off into **boy-girl pairs**.

"Okay," he told Julianna.

Mrs. Kelly plugged her MP3 player into the speakers. Then she reached down and pulled something from her bag.

"Oh no!" The kid with the curly hair smacked his forehead. "Not the straw hat!"

"Alex, shhhh . . ." Julianna warned.

Mrs. Kelly was putting on a straw farmer's hat. It looked pretty dumb on her, especially since Mrs. Kelly was wearing big earrings and a necklace.

"Mrs. Kelly takes square dancing very seriously," Julianna whispered to George.

George's eyes opened wide. "Square dancing?"

Julianna nodded. "Mrs. Kelly loves folk dances."

George gulped. That Alex kid hadn't been kidding. This was **every fourth-grade boy's worst nightmare**.

"Now, class, it's been a while since we did traditional American square dancing," Mrs. Kelly said. "So I'll demonstrate a few of the steps again. I need a partner . . ." The teacher looked around the room. "George, how about you?"

George felt his eyes bug out.

"M-me?" he asked nervously. **"I've never actually square-danced before."**

"No problem!" Mrs. Kelly exclaimed. "This will be your first lesson."

Oh man. Like it wasn't bad enough being the new kid. Now George was going to be the new kid who dances with the teacher.

"Class, this is a do-si-do," Mrs. Kelly said, folding her arms in front of her.

George folded his arms, too.

"Now we walk around each other," Mrs. Kelly told George.

George followed whatever Mrs. Kelly did. As he circled around her, **the smelly, flowery perfume she was wearing made his nose itch**. So George wrinkled and crinkled his nose up and down as he danced.

George heard somebody laugh. It probably looked like he was making faces at his teacher. But he wasn't.

"Terrific!" Mrs. Kelly said. "Now we'll try the promenade. George, you take my hand and . . ."

George didn't hear a word Mrs. Kelly said after that. All he could think about was that he was holding his teacher's hand. And Mrs. Kelly's hand was all wet and sweaty. That was really bad because **George's palms were sweating, too**. That meant he was swapping sweat with his teacher.

One by one, Mrs. Kelly did the dance moves. They had strange names like sashay, do paso, and something that sounded like almond. And George had to do them all— with his teacher!

Finally, Mrs. Kelly sent him back to be Julianna's partner. Sure, he was still going to have to square-dance. But at least Julianna was a kid.

Mrs. Kelly turned on the music. Then she began **clapping her hands** and **stomping her foot**.

"Okay, swing your partner, 'round you go," Mrs. Kelly called out to the beat of the music. "Then everybody do-si-do."

Then Mrs. Kelly did something **really weird**. She started to yodel. "Yodelay-hee-hoo."

"Now promenade your partner home," Mrs. Kelly said. "Come on now, don't let her roam."

Huh? George had already forgotten what "promenade" meant.

But Julianna knew. She grabbed George's hands and started dragging him around the gym floor.

"Allemande left, and meet your friends," Mrs. Kelly called. "Then turn around and come back again."

Now George was totally confused. Was he supposed to turn to the left? Or was he supposed to turn all the way around?

Since George wasn't sure what to do, he did both. He spun around to the left, and then . . .

Thud. George tripped and landed right on his butt.

"Oomph!" George groaned.

Some kids started laughing.

Mrs. Kelly came over. "Are you all right?" she asked.

George looked down at his untied shoe. "Yeah," he said. "I just tripped over my shoelace."

George wished the kids would stop laughing. George didn't want Mrs. Kelly to think he'd been making fun of square dancing.

But Mrs. Kelly wasn't angry. In fact, she gave George **a big, gummy smile.** "It's okay," she assured him.

"Maybe I should just sit out and watch," George suggested hopefully. "So I don't mess things up for everyone else. **I could learn a lot by watching**."

"Don't be silly," Mrs. Kelly said. "Just tie your shoelace and get ready to do-si-do."

"Yes, Mrs. Kelly," George said. He stood up and got ready to do-si-do one more time.

A few moments later, the kids were dancing again. "Eee-hah!" Mrs. Kelly kept shouting and stomping her foot. "Swing your partner 'round and 'round. Don't let those feet leave the ground."

George tried his hardest not to fall again. **Boy, Edith B. Sugarman Elementary School was definitely a strange place.**

Chapter 4

It was amazing **how hungry** do-si-doing and allemanding could make a kid. **George was starving by lunchtime.**

His mom had packed a bag lunch, but he also had money for a snack. So he followed Julianna to the food line, and got dessert. All that was left was a block of Jell-O with whipped cream on top.

George carried his tray to where the kids in class 401 were sitting. They were talking and kidding around, just the way the kids at George's old school used to. The only difference was that nobody here was shouting, **"Hey, George, over here. I saved you a seat."**

Since all the boys were on one side of the long cafeteria table, George walked over and started to sit at the end next to Louie, the kid with the cool sneakers. But a boy with red hair and freckles pushed him aside.

"Sorry, **New Kid**," the kid with red hair said. "I always sit on Louie's left at lunch. Right, Louie?"

"Right, Mike," Louie told him.

"And I always get to sit on his right," a tall, skinny kid with brown hair said. "Right, Louie?"

Louie nodded. He turned to George.

"Why don't you go sit next to your buddy?" Louie pointed to where all the girls were sitting.

There was nothing else for George to do. He sat down next to Julianna.

Julianna was eating a **slice of cafeteria pizza**. It didn't look too bad. But the girl who sat down on his other side—George heard Julianna call her Sage—had a giant-sized plate of vegetables. Before taking a bite, **she sprinkled on a whole packet of pepper**.

"Hey, Louie, want to play killer ball at recess?" the kid with red hair asked.

"What's killer ball?" George asked.

"It's this amazing game Louie made up," Mike said.

"Cool!" George said, hoping someone would say, "We'll teach you how to play." But no one did.

As the kids talked about who was on which team for killer ball, George sat quietly drinking his milk and finishing the baloney sandwich his mom had made him. **George stared at his Jell-O.**

Ooh. That dessert looked so good. But

not to eat. What George really, really wanted was to shove the whole block of Jell-O into his mouth, chew, and then slide the **chewed-up red slime** through spaces between his teeth until it dribbled down his chin.

George finished off the whipped cream, then balanced the Jell-O on his fork and was **all ready to cram it in**. But he stopped. George reminded himself that he was trying to stay out of trouble. So he dumped the Jell-O back on his plate and watched the girl next to him pour another packet of pepper onto her mountain of carrots.

George couldn't believe it. **What kind of kid liked pepper?**

Apparently, **Carrot Girl** was that kind of kid. She was already opening up a third packet of pepper when a kid returning a tray bumped her arm. Pepper flew onto George's tray.

"Ah-choo!"

The pepper made George sneeze. Two times. And the second sneeze was a big, wet one. George could feel two ropes of

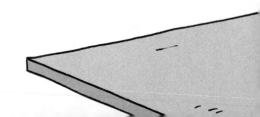

snot hanging from his nose. Quickly, he
wiped his nose on his sleeve.

But it was too late. Louie had already
seen the whole thing. "How am I
supposed to eat when I have to look at
New Kid snot?" he asked.

George was about to say sorry, but he didn't get the chance. He sneezed again. **Two ropes of snot** flew out of his nose and shot across the table—**right onto Louie's tray**.

"Ooh, gross," the girls all said. But they were laughing. So was everybody else, except Louie. Sage was laughing so hard, she looked like she was going to choke on her carrots.

Teachers never liked when there was too much laughing in school. A few giggles were okay. But not this kind of laughing. George wished the kids would stop before the grown-ups heard them.

But the cafeteria lady had already seen the commotion. And she was on her way over to George's table.

Uh-oh. Cafeteria ladies hated him.

"What's the problem here?" the cafeteria lady asked.

"The problem is my tray," Louie said. "It's got New Kid snot all over it." Louie pointed to George. "He thinks that's funny."

George couldn't believe it! Louie was making it sound like George had snotted on his tray on purpose. **But he hadn't. He'd just sneezed.**

"That's disgusting," the cafeteria lady told George. "Today you can stay here with me during recess, so we can go over some of the cafeteria rules."

"But—" George started to explain. The cafeteria lady didn't stick around to listen.

As she walked away, George stared at Louie. "It was an accident. You know that!"

Louie smiled at him. "I was just trying to help."

"Huh?" George said. Since when was squealing on someone helping?

"Now you can find out everything there is to know about the cafeteria," Louie explained. Then he got up and headed toward the door. "Okay, guys. **Time for killer ball**."

George frowned as he watched Louie. "Next time, don't do me any favors."

Chapter 5

Walking home from school was really, really lonely. **"Just me, myself, and I,"** George said. There was no one else to talk to.

Later, when his mom asked how everything went, George said, "Okay." But his mom probably could tell it hadn't been the greatest day of his life because after dinner his parents took him out for **a special first-day-of-school treat**. They went to a place called **Ernie's Ice Cream Emporium**. It was the biggest ice cream parlor George had ever seen. It took up half the block!

Ernie's was a really cool place.
Outside, there were small, metal tables
set up. Each had a cheery, red and white
striped umbrella that was open even
though it was nighttime and it wasn't
raining. Inside, there were booths with
bright red, leather benches.

"Can we sit outside?" George asked. "I
want to be able to see the sky."

That wasn't the real reason. **The real
reason was Louie.** When they had gotten
out of the car, George had spotted him
walking inside with a bunch of older
guys.

"So, how'd it go?" his dad asked as
they sat down at a table.

The last thing George wanted was a long talk about trying to "adjust." **He just wanted to enjoy his ice cream.** So he was glad that before he could answer, a girl in a black sweater and a red and white polka-dot skirt roller-skated up to the table. George smiled in spite of himself. **Roller-skating waitresses? Cool!**

"Hi," the waitress greeted George's family. "What can I get for you, folks?"

George knew exactly what he wanted.

It was the same thing he always wanted when he was bummed out. "I'll have **a root beer float**," he said. "With **two scoops of chocolate ice cream**."

"I'll have vanilla ice cream with chocolate sauce," George's mother said.

"A double rocky road sundae for me," his dad added. **"With three cherries."**

"Okay, I'll get your order for you right away," the waitress promised.

As the waitress skated off, George began to feel a little better. **There was nothing a root beer float couldn't cure.**

And his parents didn't ask any more questions, either. His mom was talking about her store—ordering glass beads, needlepoint kits, and patterns for knitting afghans. George **didn't even know what an afghan was**. He didn't want to find out.

As his mom and dad talked, George sneaked another look inside Ernie's. Louie was sitting in a window booth with the three older boys. One of them looked a lot like Louie, only taller. Maybe it was his brother.

George couldn't hear what they were saying, but it was clear that it was funny because they were all laughing really, really hard. Just the way George's friends at his old school used to laugh whenever George said something funny. **Which was pretty much all the time.**

But that was the old George. The new George didn't joke around like that. Of course, the new George didn't have any friends, either.

"It's not fun not being funny," he whispered to himself.

Just then, the waitress skated over to George's table with the tray of ice cream. "Here you go," she said as she placed a huge mug of root beer and chocolate ice cream on the table. Then she passed his mom and dad their sundaes.

"Thanks," George said. "I really needed this."

He wrapped his lips around the straw and took a huge gulp of the fizzy, sweet root beer. "Yum!"

Just then, George's dad poked him. "Whoa!" he shouted. "Look up, son!"

George did, just in time to see a
bright yellow star shoot across the night
sky.

"It's a shooting star! Quick! Make a
wish," his mom said. "And make it a good
one because **wishes on shooting stars
come true**."

George thought for a moment. "I
want to make kids laugh but not get into
trouble." he whispered. That wasn't such
a big wish. It was the kind of wish that
could come true, maybe.

George took another big gulp of his root beer float. And then another. **He couldn't drink that root beer fast enough.**

He was slurping up the last bit of it through a straw when, suddenly, George began to hear strange gurgling noises coming from the bottom of his belly. It felt like there were hundreds of tiny bubbles bouncing around in there.

The bubbles bounced up and down and all around. They ping-ponged their way from his belly to his chest, and bing-bonged their way up into his throat. And then . . .

 BUUU-U-R-P!

George let out a loud burp. He'd burped plenty of times before, but never one like this. The burp was so loud, it made the table shake. **It was so loud, his parents clapped their hands over their ears.**

The super burp was so loud that everyone sitting outside—and inside—Ernie's stopped talking and stared at George. **Then they started to laugh.** Hearing people laugh sounded just like the old days.

Then something else really strange happened. Suddenly George's hands reached across the table and grabbed two straws from the container.

It was like **his hands had a mind of their own**. George had no control over them. He watched as his hands shoved the straws up his nose. Then he jumped up on the table. It was like he was an **old-fashioned puppet** and someone had yanked him

onto the table **by his strings**.

The next thing he knew, George's hands were clapping together, pretending they were flippers.

"Look, I'm a walrus," George shouted.

A bunch of kids shot up from their seats.

"Hey, check out that kid," one of them said. He was laughing, too.

"George, get down from there!" his mother and father both shouted.

But George couldn't get down. He couldn't stop himself. **Goofiness was just bubbling out of him.**

George do-si-doed and allemanded. His parents' sundaes went flying off the table.

"George!" his mother shouted. "You just got chocolate sauce all over my new blouse."

George stuck his **right foot in**. He stuck his **right foot out**. He did the hokey pokey and he turned himself about. And then . . .

Whoooosh. It felt like a giant bubble popped inside George's stomach. All the air rushed out of him. And so did the silliness. Suddenly George didn't feel so funny anymore. He stopped dancing and looked around.

"What are you doing up there?" his father asked.

"Um . . . the hokey pokey?" George answered. He didn't know what else to say. He wasn't sure why he'd jumped up on the table. He certainly hadn't planned it. It had just happened. Right after he'd let out that giant burp.

"I'm swearing off root beer floats for good," he promised himself. **"They're too dangerous."**

Chapter 6

George went up to his room as soon as he got home from the ice cream parlor. His parents looked puzzled. **He was puzzled, too.** Something had come over him—and that was **pretty freaky** to think about.

George sat down at his new desk in his new room. His homework assignment stared back at him.

Homework on his very first day at a
new school. That just didn't seem fair.
But there it was. And the right thing to
do was work on it.

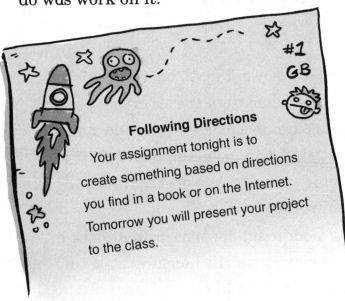

Following Directions

Your assignment tonight is to
create something based on directions
you find in a book or on the Internet.
Tomorrow you will present your project
to the class.

That didn't sound like a whole lot of
fun. In fact it sounded kind of boring.
George leaned wa-a-ay back in his chair
until the two front legs were off the
ground. It helped him to think better
that way.

Maybe the assignment didn't have to be so boring. Maybe George could turn this following directions stuff into something he could have fun with.

There were three things George loved doing. One was **telling jokes**. Another was **skateboarding**. And the third was doing **magic tricks**.

George knew skateboarding was out of the question. That wouldn't be allowed in school. And there weren't really any directions for how to be a comedian. But a magic trick could work perfectly.

That was it! George would do a magic trick for his new class.

The kids would definitely think magic was cool to do. And Mrs. Kelly would be happy because you had to follow a lot of directions to get a magic trick just right.

George went over to his bookshelf and pulled out one of his magic books. Then he flipped the pages until he found **the perfect trick**. One he'd never done before.

After tomorrow, George wasn't going to be called the new kid anymore. He was going to be **the class magician**. Things were about to change—magically.

The next morning, George carried a small carton of eggs to school. The eggs were part of his magic trick. You were supposed to hard-boil them, but George hadn't had time last night to do that. So he just made sure to **hold the eggs really, really carefully**. George wanted to make sure that nothing went wrong. Today was going to be a good day. All that weird stuff last night at Ernie's was history. Forgotten.

Or maybe not . . . When he got to his classroom, the kid with the braces—Alex—dashed over to him.

He said, "Man, **is it true what you did at Ernie's last night**?"

George put the eggs on his desk and slipped off his backpack. "Well, I-I-I. Um. Sort of," he said slowly.

"Louie told me," Alex said.

"He's telling everyone."

Louie had seen him! George looked over at Louie's desk. Sure enough, he was whispering something to Mike and Max, and pointing at George.

"It was no big deal," George said.

Alex was about to say something else when Mrs. Kelly stood up in the front of the room. "Okay, everyone," she said. "Let's take our seats."

Phew. George was never so happy to have school start. Maybe by the time he'd done his trick, everyone would be talking about what a good magician he was, and not about last night at Ernie's. **George didn't want to be famous for being the kid with the big burp** who danced on tables with straws up his nose. That was the old George.

Chapter 7

"You cover the pinecone with peanut butter," Sage explained to the class in **her soft, high voice**. "And sprinkle birdseed all over. Then you hang the pinecone on a tree and watch the birds come to feed."

George **struggled hard not to yawn**. Making a birdfeeder thing wasn't very interesting. Neither was making a Popsicle stick box, or folding a piece of paper into a cat. So far no one had a presentation that was as cool as George's magic trick was going to be.

"Very nice, Sage," Mrs. Kelly said.

"It really works, too," Sage said. "I made one and put it in a pine tree. Birds come from all over the place to feed at it."

"That must be a wonderful sight to see." Then Mrs. Kelly said, "Who would like to go next?"

George raised his hand. So did Louie.

"Okay, Louie?" Mrs. Kelly said.

Louie walked to the front of the room.

He was carrying an electric guitar.

"I'm going to play a song I learned last night," Louie told the class. "I had to follow the directions in my songbook to learn the chords."

"What is your song called?" Mrs. Kelly asked.

"It's an old rock-and-roll song called '**Louie, Louie**,'" he answered. Then he plugged in the guitar and started to play.

George hated to admit it, but **Louie's presentation was pretty cool**.

When Louie finished the song, the whole class cheered. Max and Mike stuck their fingers in their mouths and **let out loud whistles**.

Louie smiled and took a bow.

"Great job, Louie," Mrs. Kelly said. "You're becoming quite a good guitarist."

As Louie walked back to his chair, Mrs. Kelly looked over at George. "Would you like to go next?" she asked.

George put on his magician's top hat, and **strode confidently to the front of the room**, holding his egg carton in his hands.

Louie sat at his desk with his arms folded across his chest. **He stared straight at George** with a look on his face that said, "I bet this is going to be really dumb."

Well, George was going to show him!

"I'm not George today," he told the

class. "I'm **the Great Georgini**! And I'm going to perform a magic trick that will astound and amaze you."

As he spoke, **George secretly dropped a mound of salt on Mrs. Kelly's desk,** making sure no one noticed what he was doing. He quickly covered the salt with a white cloth, just like the instructions had said to do.

Then he opened a small carton of six white eggs.

"Here are six ordinary eggs," the Great Georgini continued. "There's nothing magical about them. At least not until I use magic. **When I say the magic word, the eggs will stand up all by themselves**!"

George looked out at the class. Everyone was paying attention. Except for Louie, **they all seemed really into the trick**.

George placed an egg onto the white cloth and said, "Now everybody repeat after me—Abracadabra, zing, zang, zong!"

"Abracadabra, zing, zang, zong!" the class shouted back.

George slowly let go of the egg. "Tada!" he exclaimed.

Sure enough, the egg didn't roll over. It stood there on its own. Then George repeated with the other eggs. All six looked like they were standing up straight. They were

really being held up by the pile of salt under the cloth, but the kids didn't know that.

"That's pretty awesome!" Julianna exclaimed.

"Not bad," Alex agreed.

"Magical," Sage added.

"How clever to do a magic trick. **Bravo, George**," Mrs. Kelly said with her big, gummy smile. "You have to follow directions perfectly to pull off a magic trick."

George smiled proudly. He was about to take his bow, when **suddenly he got a dizzy feeling in his head and a fizzy feeling in the pit of his stomach**. It felt like he'd just gulped down a huge root beer float—with a double scoop of chocolate ice cream.

Uh-oh.

The fizzy feeling was bing-bonging in his belly, and ping-ponging its way up into his chest. Just like it had the night before at the ice cream parlor.

Oh no! **What was happening?**

The kids were all staring at him. He opened his mouth. But all that came out was . . .

Mrs. Kelly gasped. **This was no ordinary burp.** This was a supercolossal burp that blew papers off his teacher's desk. The kind of burp you could probably hear all the way from the moon!

Quickly, George started to cover his mouth. He wanted to say excuse me. But that's not what he did. **Not at all.**

Instead, George's hands began
acting up again. Just like last night!
They picked up the six eggs, and began
to juggle. That would have been really
cool—except for one thing. **George
had no idea how
to juggle.**

Crack. Splat. Yuck!

One by one, the eggs smashed onto the floor in **a gooey mess**. George frowned. Boy, it had really been a mistake not to hard-boil them the way the magic book said.

George knew that what he should do right now was clean up the mess as fast as possible. But his feet seemed to have other ideas. They wanted to **skid across the floor on the trail of egg slime**. So that was what George did . . . *wheee!* Then he turned around, opened his arms wide, and took a bow.

The kids were all clapping wildly. **But Mrs. Kelly wasn't.**

Whoosh. Suddenly George felt a huge bubble pop inside his stomach. All the air rushed right out of him. And so did all the silliness.

George wanted to say, "Whoops. I didn't mean to do that." So he opened his mouth and . . . those were exactly the words that came out of his mouth.

George looked at his teacher's face. **He had seen that look lots of times.** George was in big trouble, again.

Chapter 8

"I've heard about this boy," Mr. Coleman, the school janitor, said to Mrs. Kelly as he walked into the classroom with his mop and pail. "He's the one who caused that **ruckus** in the **cafeteria**."

George hadn't done anything wrong in the cafeteria. He'd just sneezed. But there was no point in arguing. **He was in enough trouble already.**

"Here," Mr. Coleman said to George. He shoved the mop into George's hands. "You made the mess. You clean up the mess."

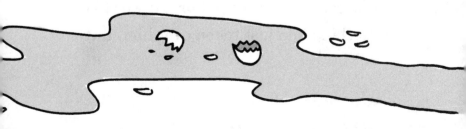

"Yes, sir," he said. George began moving the wet mop over the gooey raw egg goop.

Swish. Swish. Swish. The sound of the moving mop was pretty much all George heard. It was very quiet in the room. The rest of the class had already gone to lunch. It was just George, Mr. Coleman, and Mrs. Kelly. **Two adults to one kid.**

"George, I understand that it's very hard to come into a new school, especially after the school year has started," Mrs. Kelly told him. "And I can tell you're a bright boy. But clowning around is not a good way to get to know everyone. **You need to try and use some self-control**."

George wanted to tell his teacher that he'd been trying really hard to control himself. The whole egg thing hadn't been in his control. After the burp, it was like something had just taken over him. But

how do you explain something like that to a teacher? Especially when George couldn't even explain it to himself.

Grumble. Rumble. George heard his stomach rumble. But he understood that he wasn't going to lunch until every drop of egg slime was cleaned up.

What George didn't understand was what had made him try to juggle the eggs. He hadn't planned on it. It wasn't part of the trick. It had just happened. He'd let out that giant burp, and then **everything went out of control**. Just like it had at Ernie's Ice Cream Emporium the night before.

George thought back to the night before. He'd seen the **shooting star**, made that wish about wanting to make kids laugh, and then along came the super burp and suddenly he was clowning around like crazy . . .

George smacked his forehead. That was it! **His wish had come true.** But it had also gone wrong . . . The part about not getting into trouble hadn't come true at all. **It was like that part of the wish had been cut off or something.**

George had wanted to be the one deciding when to fool around. But he wasn't. It was all up to the super burp!

That big, giant burp made him do stuff he didn't want to do. Goofy things. Bad stuff. Stuff that got George in trouble.

It was no ordinary burp. It was a magic super burp. **And it was ba-a-ad.**

George was really starving by the time the floor was cleaned up. He knew he had to hurry if he was going to get to the cafeteria in time for lunch.

There was only one problem. George couldn't remember where the cafeteria was. Julianna had taken him there yesterday because she was his buddy. But today he was on his own. And he was totally lost.

Then **George smelled something**— the familiar scent of spoiled milk, boiled hot dogs, and Jell-O. The smell of **school lunch**! All George had to do was follow his nose and he'd be in the cafeteria in no time.

Chapter 9

That afternoon after school, George hung out by himself. Again. But at least he had his skateboard—and his new **skateboard ramp**. His dad had built it for him near the loading dock behind his mom's store. The ramp led into an empty alleyway with no traffic. George could skate there as much as he wanted. **It was perfect.**

George tried to focus all of his attention on his skateboarding. He was good at controlling his moves on the board. A lot better than he was at

controlling the super burp, anyway. That thing had a mind of its own.

George pushed any thoughts of that stupid burp out of his head, and continued working on his ollie. The idea was to pop the skateboard up in the air and then land smoothly on the ground. George was determined to become **Grand Master of the Ollie**.

George stood at the top of his steep ramp. He pushed off, and then soared down the slope of the alleyway. Once he was going pretty fast, he put his back foot on the tail of his board and pushed down. At the same time, he slid his other foot forward. And then . . .

Wheee! George and the skateboard flew up into the air. It stayed there for a second. **George felt like he was flying.**

A moment later, the board landed on the ground, and George rolled down the alleyway, with his legs crouched, his arms spread for balance, and his mouth smiling.

"Yes!" George exclaimed. He pumped his fist into the air.

"Hey, that was cool!"

George turned around, surprised.

"You're pretty good," the kid said. He had short, blond hair and was wearing a T-shirt with a bolt of lightning on the front.

George stared at him. Pretty good? That had been a perfect ollie. A work of art.

"I'm also learning to do a 180-degree ollie," George told him. "The whole skateboard turns right around in midair."

"Cool," the kid said. "You looked like you were flashing across the sky. **Like a bolt of lightning**."

George smiled. "Thanks."

"Or the Green Lantern, or the Human Fly," the kid continued. **"I'm Chris**. I was on my way to the comic book store on the corner. I heard the noise back here."

"I'm George," George replied. **"I'm new here."**

"Yeah. I know."

George frowned. Had this kid already heard about the eggs-perience in the classroom? Or the table dancing at Ernie's? Or blowing snot on Louie's lunch?

But Chris didn't bring up any of those things. Instead, he just said, "I'm in Mrs. Miller's fourth-grade class."

"I have Mrs. Kelly," George said.

"So, how do you like the school?" Chris asked.

George shrugged. "I guess **Edith B. Boogerman Elementary School's** okay."

Chris laughed. "Boogerman. That's funny."

George looked at Chris strangely. He couldn't believe no one had ever called it that before. It was such an easy joke!

George smiled. This Chris kid seemed pretty nice. And he thought George was funny. Best of all, they went to the same school and were in the same grade. If Chris stuck around for a while longer, **this could officially count as hanging out with somebody**.

Chapter 10

Chris lived just a block away from George. So the next morning, George and Chris walked to school together.

Chris told George about a comic book he was writing. "I made up this superhero called **Toiletman**. His secret weapon is a toilet plunger. And he carries a roll of magic toilet paper to tie up the bad guys."

"Sounds good," George said.

Then he smiled. "Do you know what one toilet said to the other toilet?"

"What?" Chris asked.

"You look a little flushed." George laughed at his own joke.

Chris laughed, too. "Hey, can I use that in my comic book?"

"Sure," George said. "**Maybe I can help with your comic**. I know lots of jokes."

The boys had just reached the schoolyard when they saw Alex.

George waved to him. Then he flipped up his skateboard with one foot and grabbed it with his hand.

George was proud of his board. It was red and black with **a really spooky painting of a bat skeleton** in the middle.

"That's the coolest board I've ever seen," Alex said.

"Thanks," George said. "You can try it if you want."

"I've seen him on his skateboard," Chris told Alex. "He's amazing."

George smiled.

Just then, Louie walked over. "You guys want to play **killer ball** before school?" he asked Chris and Alex.

Alex shook his head. "Later maybe," he told Louie. **"I want to try out George's skateboard."**

"I bet you can't even ride that thing," Louie said to George.

George just smiled. He didn't have to prove he could skateboard. **He knew he could.**

Just then the bell rang. It was time to go inside.

"Saved by the bell, huh, New Kid?" Louie said.

George pretended not to hear Louie. He picked up his skateboard and walked into the school building.

I'll show you, George thought to himself.

Just not right this minute.

Chapter 11

"We have gym class after this," Alex whispered to George as the class worked on their math sheets that morning. **"I hope Mr. Trainer's back."**

"Me too," George whispered. Otherwise he'd have to do-si-do and promenade again. That hadn't gone so well the first time.

They both stopped talking and went back to their math sheets because Mrs. Kelly was going around the room checking the kids' work. **She was only one row away.**

Suddenly, George felt a little bubble inside—kind of like he was going to burp.

"Here comes **Mrs. Smelly**," he said.

Oops. The words had just popped out of his mouth. He hadn't meant to say them. Although the name fit. Mrs. Kelly's perfume was really smelly.

Now the bubbles started to ping-pong around. All on their own. George's eyes crossed and his tongue hung out.

"That perfume is gonna make me pass out."

Oh no! Those words had come out all on their own, too. And the bubbles were getting stronger.

George held his breath, trying to force the burp down. But Alex had heard everything and was laughing. Mrs. Kelly seemed to know it was George who had made Alex laugh.

Please, not now. No magic burp, George thought to himself.

"Alex! George!" Mrs. Kelly scolded. She was not smiling her gummy smile now. "**I had no idea double-digit multiplication was that funny.** Do you want to share the joke with the rest of the class?"

Alex stopped laughing really fast. "No," he told her. "Sorry."

George just kept holding his breath. He shook his head, but didn't open his mouth. Then, a second later, he felt as if a bubble gum bubble went *pop!* inside him. Yessss! **George had squelched the belch!**

In the gym, a huge black-and-white soccer ball came rolling toward George. It was just like a regular soccer ball, only huge. **Like a soccer ball for giants.** It was the biggest ball George had ever seen.

A tall, skinny man with dark brown hair and a moustache was behind the rolling ball. He was wearing shorts and had a whistle around his neck. George figured he had to be Mr. Trainer, the gym teacher.

"We're playing **crab soccer**," Julianna explained. "It's just like regular soccer, except you sit down while you're playing."

Julianna sat down with her feet flat on the floor. She placed her hands on the floor with her fingers facing outward. Then she lifted her body and began to walk on her hands and feet.

George laughed. **She did sort of look like a crab.**

"Now you try it," Julianna urged George.

George tried to copy what Julianna was doing. But **it wasn't so easy moving his hands and feet at the same time**. He wasn't going nearly as fast as Julianna was.

"Our team is trying to get the ball in the goal over there," Julianna said. She

pointed across the gym.

Mr. Trainer blew his whistle. The kids all began crab crawling around the floor.

Alex kicked the ball really hard. It was headed right for the goal. But Louie was a quick crab. He blocked the ball, and kicked it back toward the other side of the gym.

"Go Louie!" Max shouted.

"Nice save!" Mike cheered.

George scrambled to get in front of the ball so he could kick it away. But **then it happened. Again.** Something started to bubble up in George's belly. It was stronger than it had been in math class.

The bubbles were already ping-ponging around in his stomach and threatening to move up into his chest. He'd done it once before. Now he had to do it again. **He had to beat the burp!**

Quickly, George shut his lips tight, trying to lock the bubbles in and then he flipped over and did a handstand against the wall. The bubbles were still trying to escape. But now George was upside down. If the

bubbles moved up, they'd go into his feet. There was no way out from there!

"Young man!" Mr. Trainer cried out. "What are you doing?"

George didn't know what to say. He couldn't exactly tell his gym teacher that he was trying to squelch a belch!

"George! Watch out!" Julianna shouted suddenly.

Upside down, George saw the huge soccer ball careening across the gym floor.

It was coming straight at George's head!

Quickly, George flipped over. He landed on his rear end and then kicked the oncoming ball as hard as he could.

Bam! The giant crab soccer ball went soaring across the room.

"Goal!" Mr. Trainer shouted.

"Awesome kick!" Julianna said.

Out of the corner of his eye, George could see Louie. **He looked really mad.** George had a feeling he was the one who had kicked the ball right at his head.

But that didn't really matter to George. Neither did how far he'd kicked the giant crab soccer ball. Or that **his team was ahead**.

George was just happy he'd won out over the super burp.

At least for now.

Chapter 12

At lunch, George sat with Chris, Alex, and Julianna. They were pretty nice kids. And not once, for the rest of the day, did George feel even one bubble in his belly. All through recess and art class he felt **100 percent like an ordinary kid**.

Art class had been especially fun because the kids were starting to make their papier-mâché piñatas. George loved sloshing around in the **soupy, goopy, papier-mâché paste** as he built his piñata.

In fact, he was having so much fun that he didn't even get mad when Mike told him his skateboard piñata looked like a big, white tongue. Which it absolutely did not.

George was actually feeling pretty good about things when the bell for dismissal rang. And then he heard Louie calling him.

"Hey, New Kid. Are you ready to show us what a hot skateboarder you are?"

Louie was mocking George. **But so what?**

"Sure. Meet me outside," George told Louie.

"Yeah right," Louie said. "You'll probably sneak out the back entrance."

Mike and Max laughed.

George frowned. **What did Louie expect him to do?** Skateboard right here in the hallway?

George put his backpack and his skateboard on the floor. Then he started

to put on his helmet so he would be ready
to skate as soon as he got outside. As
he was buckling his helmet strap under
his chin, George got a strange feeling in
his stomach. A bunch of bubbles were
suddenly bouncing up and down and all
around in his belly.

Oh no! Not again!

George tried desperately to stop the bubbles. He held his nose and clamped his mouth shut. But the bubbles were strong. He'd kept them down before, but George wasn't sure he could do it again.

"George, what's wrong?" Alex asked. **"Your face is turning purple."**

The bubbles ping-pong-pinged their way up out of George's stomach.

They boing-bing-boinged their way to his chest.

They bing-boing-binged their way up his throat. And then . . .

George let out the **loudest burp** in the **history of Edith B. Sugarman Elementary School**. In fact, it was possibly the loudest burp ever burped in the history of all elementary schools. A super-duper mega burp! The burps at the ice cream shop and in his classroom were **baby burps** compared to this one.

Suddenly all the talking in the hallway stopped. Everyone turned to stare at George.

"It wasn't me!" George declared.

But **there was no hiding it**. George was the big burper. Everyone had heard it. Now everyone was laughing.

And then suddenly, George's feet wanted to jump on his skateboard right here in the middle of the school. George tried to stop them by grabbing onto Alex's shoulder.

"Are you okay?" Alex asked.

George couldn't stop himself. The super burp had taken over. He tried to keep holding onto Alex. But all at once his hands let go. They weren't cooperating.

And neither were his feet. They leaped onto the board. And before he knew what was happening, **George was rolling down the halls**.

He shifted his weight to the back of the board and . . . *wheee!* He took off into the air and turned the board around in a circle. **A perfect 180!**

"Satisfied?" George shouted as he passed by Louie.

"George!" Mrs. Kelly came racing out of the classroom. "Get off that skateboard right now!"

But George didn't get off. He couldn't.
It was like his feet were cemented to the board.

"Woo-hoo!" George shouted as he popped up into the air in another ollie.

Kids started clapping and whistling.

"Check this out!" George called to the kids. He turned the corner ready to do an awesome **pop shove-it**.

George looked over his shoulder. He could see Mr. Trainer running after him.

"I'll put a stop to this!" Mr. Trainer shouted to Mrs. Kelly. But George was too fast for him.

Practically every kid at Edith B. Sugarman Elementary School was trailing after **George and his runaway skateboard**. George jumped up and landed back down on the skateboard.

As he passed her office, the principal came running out into the hall. "George

Brown! There is no skateboarding allowed in school!" she shouted as he whizzed by.

George knew that. The principal didn't understand. The burp was in control, not George. He turned his head and tried to say, "I'm sorry." But nothing came out.

"George! **Watch out**!" someone shouted. George thought it sounded like Alex.

When George turned back around, he saw what the problem was. He was **heading straight for the art room** at the end of the hallway. The door was open. George was going too fast to stop. Besides, the magic burp wouldn't let him.

"Whoa!" he shouted as he whizzed into the room and smashed into a table.

Ride over.

Whoosh. Suddenly George felt a big

bubble pop right in the middle of his stomach. The air just rushed right out of him.

The super burp had disappeared. But George was still here, left to deal with the mess.

He fell off his skateboard and landed on his rear end just as a pail of **icky,**

sticky, papier-mâché goo tipped over. Yucky, white papier-mâché rained down over George's head.

George sat there, feeling the slippery, ooey-gooey, white paste **slither down his neck**, and ooze down under his shirt. It dripped on George's face and into his mouth. Blech. It was the most disgusting

thing George had ever tasted. And considering he'd once mixed **tuna fish with chocolate ice cream and ketchup**, that was saying a lot.

"Hey, check it out," Alex said. "George is a human piñata."

The kids were all crowding in the doorway.

"Nice job, New Kid," Louie said in a mean voice.

George sighed. New Kid. **There were those two words again.**

"You're in some mess now," Louie told George.

George sat there for a minute, staring up at Louie. He didn't say a word. What could he say? **Louie was right.**

"George!" Mrs. Kelly exclaimed as she ran into the art room. "Why would you do that? Just what got into you?"

George sighed. It was actually what

had gotten out of him that had made him act all goofy. But **what was he supposed to say**? The burp made me do it? That would just get him into more trouble.

More trouble was the last thing George needed.

Chapter 13

That afternoon, George walked home alone—again. He'd had to stay after school to clean up the art room. That had taken a really long time since the principal wouldn't let Chris or Alex stay to help. By the time he'd finished, all the kids had gone home.

Well, **one thing was for sure**. No one was going to call George the new kid anymore. **Everyone knew his name**—including the art teacher, the janitor, and the school principal, Mrs. McKeon. He'd spent a lot of time talking to her before she let him go home.

George reached up and scratched at his head. The papier-mâché paste was starting to harden in his hair. **It was all clumped behind his ears, too.** He was going to have to take a really long shower tonight. **Then he'd have to clean up the dirty tub.**

And after that, his parents would talk about being responsible. George could just hear his mother asking, "What happened to the new George?"

Worst of all, his parents would probably take away his skateboard for a week or two.

Why me? George thought as he walked through Beaver Brook on his way home. Of all the millions of kids on the planet, why am I the one to get stuck with this stupid, magic super burp? It didn't seem fair.

George had a feeling **he hadn't seen the last of the burp**. It was going to come back. But who knew when? All George knew for sure was that he would have to work hard to stop it when it did. Because if he let that burp out, there was no telling what might happen next!

George Brown, CLASS CLOWN

Trouble
Magnet

by Nancy Krulik
illustrated by Aaron Blecha

Grosset & Dunlap
An Imprint of Penguin Group (USA) Inc.

Chapter 1

"Okay, this is just wrong," George Brown whispered to his friend Alex. They were in the school gym, watching their fourth-grade teacher, Mrs. Kelly, do a hula dance.

"*Seriously* wrong," Alex agreed. **"Teachers shouldn't hula-hula dance."**

Mrs. Kelly gave the class **a big, gummy smile**. A little piece of green food was caught between her teeth.

"This move is called *'Ami 'Oniu*," Mrs. Kelly said, swaying back and forth in a figure eight.

It's embarrassing when your teacher
is dancing in the middle of the gym floor
with a grass skirt over her pants and a
paper flower necklace around her neck.
But George didn't even crack a smile. He
knew better. Mrs. Kelly took her dancing
really seriously. It wouldn't be nice to
laugh. And George was trying really hard
to be a nice, well-behaved fourth-grader.
**His days of being the class clown were
over.**

"Hula dances tell a story," Mrs. Kelly
told the class. She straightened her
crooked, black glasses. "The dance I'm
doing now is about catching fish in the
ocean."

Mrs. Kelly moved her arms up and
down like waves in the ocean. The skin
on the back of her arms wiggled and
jiggled as she waved. The wiggly,
jiggly skin kept on waving, even after

Mrs. Kelly stopped moving. George knew he shouldn't stare, but he couldn't help himself. **It was too gross to ignore.**

"Oh, we're going to a Hukilau," Mrs. Kelly began to sing in a high-pitched voice. She wiggled her hips and jiggled her arms. "Huki, huki, lau . . ."

The kids all stared at their teacher. This was pretty hard to believe.

"Okay, class," Mrs. Kelly called out. "Now comes the fun part. **Make up your own hula dances.** Use your bodies to tell stories."

Nobody moved.

"Come on, it's fun," Mrs. Kelly said. "Huki, huki, hukilau."

One by one, the kids began to move around. They weren't hula dances. But they were dances that told stories. *Sort of.*

Sage began stretching her arms out like tree branches. "I'm a tree reaching toward the sun."

George rolled his eyes. That was really cheesy. But, of course, he didn't say that. Teachers hated when you made fun of other kids.

Louie, who thought he was the coolest kid in the fourth grade, rocked out on an **air guitar**. As he played, he made twanging noises. "Twang a lang-lang-lang."

"Rock on, Louie!" his friend Mike cheered.

"Twang! Twang!" Louie sang even louder.

Julianna swung an imaginary bat at an imaginary baseball.

"And it's outta here!"
she shouted.

George hunched over and began
swinging his arms. **He was an ape looking
for a banana.**

But before he really got started dancing,
George felt something funny in his

stomach. It was like there were hundreds of tiny bubbles bouncing around inside him. Then **strange gurgling noises** started coming from the bottom of his belly.

There was a big burp inside him. And it really wanted to come out! But there was no way George was going to let it. Not here. Not now. Because his burps were magic and caused trouble with a capital *T*.

This burp was strong. George could already feel it bing-bonging its way out of his belly and ping-ponging its way into his chest. He had to stop it!

George dropped down to the floor on his belly. He started wriggling up and down like a giant, slithering snake. George didn't care what he looked like. He would do anything to bump that burp back down. He pinched his nose and clamped his mouth shut.

Stay down, burp, George ordered. *I*

mean it. Stay down.

"Wow, George, look at you!" Mrs. Kelly said. "What kind of story are you trying to tell us?"

George gulped. There was definitely a story behind the dance he was doing. It just wasn't one he could tell his teacher. No way! The super burps were **George's secret**. And he was going to keep it that way.

Chapter 2

It had all started on George's first day at Edith B. Sugarman Elementary School. George's dad was in the army, and his family moved around a lot. So here they were living in Beaver Brook, and once again George was at a new school. By now, George knew that when you're the new kid, you expect the first day to be rotten. **But *this* first day was the rottenest.**

George had promised himself to turn over a new leaf. **No more pranks.** No more class clown. He wasn't going to get into any trouble anymore, like he had at all his old schools. And at first, it had really worked. He'd raised his hand before answering questions. He didn't make faces behind teachers' backs. And when Mrs. Kelly made him be her square-dancing partner, **George hadn't made a joke**. Not even when his teacher put on a straw hat and started yodeling.

By the end of that first day, George had the exact same number of friends he'd had at the beginning of the day. **Zero.** Being the new, well-behaved George was no fun.

That night, George's parents took him out to Ernie's Ice Cream Emporium. While they were sitting outside and George was finishing his root beer float, a shooting star flashed across the sky. So George made a wish.

I want to make kids laugh—but not get into trouble.

The trouble was the star was gone

before George could finish the wish. So only half came true—the first half.

A minute later, George had a **funny feeling in his belly.** It was like there were hundreds of tiny **bubbles** bouncing around in there. The bubbles bounced up and down and all around. **They ping-ponged their way into his chest** and bing-bonged their way up into his throat. And then . . .

George let out a big burp. A *huge* burp. A SUPER burp!

The super burp was loud, and it was *magical.*

Suddenly George lost control of his arms and legs. It was like they had minds of their own. His hands grabbed straws and stuck them up his nose like a walrus. His feet jumped up on the table and **started dancing the hokey pokey**. Everyone at Ernie's started laughing—except his parents.

Now every time the burp came, trouble followed. ***Plenty of trouble.*** George never knew when a burp would strike or what it would make him do. Like juggle raw eggs in his classroom or skateboard right into a bucket of papier-

mâché goo in the art room. Every time
the burp came, George made the other
kids laugh. But he also managed to make
grown-ups really mad.

That was why, at the moment, George
was on the floor wriggling
his body up and down
like a snake.

It was why he was holding his breath and almost turning blue. George wasn't trying to make fun of hula dancing. He was just trying to keep the super burp down.

Whoosh. Suddenly George felt a huge bubble pop inside his stomach. All the air rushed right out of him. **The fizzy feeling was gone.**

All right! George had beaten the burp! He leaped to his feet and pumped his fist in the air.

"George?" Mrs. Kelly asked again. "Please tell us what your dance is about."

Uh-oh. How was he going to explain this one? "Well . . . um . . . I'm a snake," George told her. "And . . . I'm excited . . . because I just swallowed a rat. Whole."

"Ooh, gross," Sage said.

"Snakes do eat rats," George told her. "We learned that at my old school."

Mrs. Kelly flashed George one of her huge, gummy smiles. "You're right," she said. "Some snakes do eat rats. That was a very original hula dance, George."

George was glad his teacher had liked his dance. But he hoped he'd never have to do that—or any other belch-squelching dances—again. He hoped the super burp was gone for good.

But somehow he doubted it.

Chapter 3

George saw the sign the minute he and the other fourth-graders walked into the cafeteria at lunch time.

"Cool," George said. **"A talent show."**

"I painted the poster," his friend Chris said.

"Who's the creepy-looking lady on it?" George asked.

"That's supposed to be **Edith B. Sugarman**," Chris told him. Then he asked, "So? Are you going to sign up for the talent show?"

George shrugged. "I guess."

"You're not going to skateboard again, are you, George?" Louie said really loudly, so everyone would hear.

Mike and Max, who were like Louie's shadows, started to laugh.

George made a face. Skateboarding in the school hallway hadn't been his fault. But of course he couldn't tell Louie that. Louie would never believe there was such a thing as a magic super burp. Who would?

"Maybe we could be superheroes," Chris suggested to George and Alex. "I could be Spiderman. Alex could be

Superman. And, George, you could be Batman."

Chris had more superhero comic books than anybody George had ever known.

He was even writing
his own comic book
about a superhero
he'd made up,
Toiletman.

"What would
we *do* as superheroes?" Alex asked.
"Just stand onstage in old Halloween
costumes?"

"We could attach ourselves to wires,
and some of the other kids could pull us
up into the air," Chris told him. **"That
would be really cool."**

George wasn't so sure. What if the
wires broke? No way George wanted to
go from Batman to Splatman in front of
the whole school.

George sat down at the lunch table.
Chris and Alex sat on either side of him.

"What did your mom pack today?"
Alex asked George.

George peeked into his lunch bag. **"A baloney sandwich,"** he said. "And a banana."

"I got ham and cheese," Chris said. "And a bag of peanuts."

"I have egg salad," Alex told the boys. "Anyone want to trade?"

George and Chris shook their heads.

"I know. Egg salad is the worst," Alex admitted, sniffing his sandwich. "It kind of **smells like the bathroom** after my dad's been in there a long time."

George and Chris laughed. They knew exactly what he meant.

George looked down at his baloney sandwich. For a minute, he thought

about poking holes in two balogney slices and putting them over his face like a mask. **That would totally crack Chris and Alex up.** Chris would probably call George *Baloneyman* or something.

But as George peeled off the baloney slices, he caught a glimpse of the cafeteria lady.

She was staring right at him.

Cafeteria ladies definitely didn't like masks made out of baloney slices. They took food really seriously.

Besides, baloney masks were something the old George would make. The new and improved George didn't play with his food. So George closed his sandwich up again and took a bite.

"There's a game of **killer ball** going on," Alex said as he, Chris, and George went out to the school yard for recess. "You guys want to play?"

Killer ball was a game Louie had invented. It was kind of like dodgeball.

"We always lose," Chris said.

"Because we're never on Louie's team," Alex told him.

The boys watched as Louie clobbered Julianna on the back with a soccer ball.

"Ouch!" Julianna shouted. "You didn't have to throw it so hard."

"See?" Alex said.

Chris popped some of his peanuts into his mouth.

Just then, two chattering squirrels ran right past the boys and up a tree. George was about to suggest that they throw the squirrels a few peanuts. But before he could even open his mouth, he felt **a strange bubbling** in the bottom of his belly. Maybe it was the baloney sandwich . . . *or maybe it wasn't.*

Oh man! Not again.

George tried desperately to stop the bubbles. He held his nose and clamped his mouth shut.

"George, what are you doing?" Chris asked him.

George didn't answer. He was afraid to talk. **Those bubbles were strong.**

George had already kept one inside today. But this one seemed determined to get out.

The bubbles ping-pong-pinged their way up out of George's stomach.

They boing-bing-boinged their way to his chest.

They bing-boing-binged their way up his throat. And then . . .

George let out a supersonic burp! It was so loud, it made the leaves on the trees shake. Kids clear across the playground could hear it.

"**Whoaaaa!**" Alex exclaimed.

"**Impressive!**" Chris added.

George opened his mouth and tried to

say, "Excuse me." But those weren't
the words that came out. Instead, he said,
"You know how you catch a squirrel? You
climb a tree and act like a nut!"

And with that, George's feet started
running toward the nearest tree. George
tried to make his legs go stiff so they
couldn't climb. He hugged the trunk of
the tree and tried to stay on the ground.
But his arms and legs had their own
ideas. They wanted to climb that tree.
And the next thing he knew, that's
exactly what George was doing.

"**George Brown**, get down from
there!" Mrs. Kelly called out. **"You'll hurt
yourself."**

George wanted to get down. He really
did. But his feet wouldn't let him. Up, up,
up he climbed.

"Squeak! Squeak!" George chattered
to a squirrel on a branch. But the

**squirrel didn't understand George's
squirrel-speak**. It scampered away as fast
as it could.

George's cheeks wanted to have a little
squirrely fun. They sucked in a lot of air
and blew themselves up like a big balloon.
Now George looked like a squirrel storing
nuts in his cheeks. Sort of, anyway.

"Is he trying to catch a squirrel?"
George heard Chris ask.

"He's **definitely acting nutty**," Alex
agreed. They were both laughing really
hard.

By now the principal, Mrs. McKeon, had
come out onto the playground.

"George Brown, there is **no climbing
trees during recess**!" she called up to him.
"You know that!"

George *did* know that. Unfortunately, the super burp didn't. And neither did his hands. They weren't about to let his cheeks have all the fun. Before George knew what was happening, his fists were drumming on his chest.

"AHAHAHAHAHA!" George let out a yell. He was no ordinary squirrel. He was a Tarzan squirrel.

"George!" Mrs. McKeon shouted angrily. **"Get down this minute!"**

"AHAHAHAHAHA!" George shouted even louder. His arms reached out toward a long, thin branch. His feet got ready to push off so he could swing to the next tree.

Whoosh. Suddenly George felt **something pop in his stomach**. It was like someone had punctured a balloon. All the air rushed out of him. The super burp was gone!

But George was still up in the tree.

George looked down at the ground. **Whoa! He was really high up.** He grabbed the tree trunk and held on tight.

"Get down from there right now, young man," Mrs. McKeon shouted.

"Yes, ma'am," George said. Slowly, he began to climb down the tree.

Mrs. McKeon and Mrs. Kelly were both waiting for George when he reached the ground.

"I'm so disappointed, George," Mrs. Kelly said. She straightened her glasses and wiped the **little beads of sweat** from under her nose. "You know the recess rules."

"What got into you?" Mrs. McKeon asked him.

George frowned. It wasn't what got

into him that made him act so crazy. It was what slipped *out* of him. **That super burp was really *ba-a-ad!***

"Um . . . I don't know, ma'am," George said. He looked down at the ground.

"I suggest you save your squirrel act for the talent show," Mrs. McKeon told him. "You know the way to my office. Now march!"

George sighed and followed the principal. Another recess sitting in the gray, metal chair that made **your butt fall asleep**. Another recess sitting listening to Mrs. McKeon's pen scratching against the papers on her desk.

Another recess staring out the window while the other kids got to play.

Chapter 4

"I'm going to act out a scene from my comic book," Chris said as he, Alex, and George walked to school the next morning. "My mom said I can use **an old toilet plunger and a toilet seat for my sword and shield**."

"Cool," George said.

"I'm signing up to work backstage," Alex said. "I don't have any talent. At least not the kind you perform in a talent show."

George understood what his friend meant. Alex was good at math and science. But you couldn't stand up in front of an audience and do long division.

Working backstage wasn't such a bad idea. Teachers really liked when you helped out with things like that. Maybe if he did that, Mrs. Kelly might forgive him for recess yesterday.

"Maybe I'll work backstage with you," George told Alex.

"Awesome," Alex said. "They need a lot of help with the curtains and the lights and stuff."

George didn't want to just work backstage. He did have some talent show talents. **He wanted to do an act, too. He just didn't know what kind. Not yet.**

All morning, George couldn't help thinking about the talent show. While the class was working on their grammar worksheets, George pictured himself singing to the crowd. Unfortunately, George wasn't a great singer. And a minute later, he pictured the crowd throwing squishy tomatoes at his head.

During math, while part of his brain was busy working on multiplication problems, the other part was thinking about a stand-up comedy routine. He knew a lot of really funny jokes like the one he e-mailed last night to his old friend Kevin back in Cherrydale: *How can you tell if an elephant's been in your refrigerator? You find his footprint in the peanut butter.*

George laughed quietly at his own joke. But apparently not quietly enough.

"George!" Mrs. Kelly scolded. "Can you tell me what's so funny about this math problem?"

"N-n-nothing," George said.

"I'm going to read this poem called 'Casey at the Bat,'" Julianna said at lunch. "It's all about **this amazing baseball player**. Well, he's amazing until the end of the poem, anyway. Then he strikes out."

"Ariella, Tess, Molly, and I are rehearsing our dance after school today," Sage said. "We have the music picked out already. It's called the Four Seasons."

"What are we gonna do, Louie?" Max asked.

Louie looked at him. "We're gonna start a band and the talent show will be our first gig," he said. "I'm on guitar and Mike's on drums."

Max frowned. "I don't play anything," he said. "How am I supposed to be in the band?"

Louie thought about that for a minute. Finally he said, "You can be the roadie."

"Cool!" Max said. Then he stopped and gave Louie a confused look. "What's a roadie?" he asked.

"A roadie is the guy who sets up equipment," George told him. "He also gets the sandwiches and sodas and stuff."

Louie shot George a look that said, *Who asked you?*

"I can play stuff," George told Louie, Mike, and Max. "At my old school, I learned to play tuba and . . ."

Louie burst out laughing. "Tuba?" he

asked. "Are you kidding? Whoever heard of a tuba in a rock band?"

"Not me," Mike and Max said at the same time.

"Let me finish," George said. "I also play keyboard. I was in a rock band at my old school. We were **Slinky and the Worms**."

"That's a dumb name," Louie said.

"Look, maybe I could play keyboard for you," George told him.

Alex and Chris were looking at George

as if he were out of his mind. He could practically hear them thinking, *Why would George want to play in a band with Louie?*

George was sort of asking himself the same question. But Louie was starting a band. And even though George could have played keyboard on his own during the talent show, that wouldn't be as cool as being in a band. Besides, playing alone meant everybody in the audience could tell when you

made a mistake. In a band it was much harder to figure out who was messing up.

Louie looked at him strangely. "Why would I want you on keyboard?" he asked.

"Because guitar and drums don't make much of a band," George explained.

It was hard for Louie to argue with that. "Well, how do I know you can play?" he asked finally.

"Yeah, you could be making this whole Slinky the Worm thing up," Max added.

"Slinky *and* the Worms," George corrected him. "And I'm not making it up."

"Prove it," Louie said. "Come to my house. Then I'll decide if you're good enough to be in the band.

"Anytime you want," George replied.

Louie stood up. "Okay, I'm done eating," Louie said, pushing his tray away. "Time for some killer ball."

"I'm done, too," Mike said.

"Me three," Max agreed.

Louie, Max, and Mike started to walk out of the cafeteria. But before they did, Louie turned around. "Oh, and one more thing," he told George. "I'm lead singer."

Suddenly, George felt a little bubble brewing up inside—kind of like he was going to burp. He opened his mouth to say, "Okay." But out came a little burp. And then he said, "You should sing solo. *So low* no one can hear you."

Chris and Alex started to laugh.

"What did you say?" Louie asked.

George didn't answer. That had been **a mini-magic burp**. The next one might be a whopper.

"He said that he thought so," Chris told Louie. "I heard him."

"Yeah, that's what I figured he said," Louie said. But he didn't sound like he really believed it.

George shot Chris **a closed-mouth smile**. But he didn't say a thing. He was afraid to open his mouth.

When Louie was gone, Chris asked, "How come you want to be in Louie's band?"

"Being in a band is cool," George said.

"Yeah, I guess," Alex agreed. "If I could play guitar, I'd be in a band."

It would have been great to be in a band with Chris and Alex. But since that wasn't going to happen, George would have to settle for being in Louie's band.

George watched through the cafeteria window. Louie really **nailed a third-grader** in killer ball.

Gulp. What if Louie played just as hard at killer *band*?

Chapter 5

"Okay, class, get ready to go to the library," Mrs. Kelly announced the next morning to the kids in class 401. "We're going to do some research on your fiftieth state projects."

"Which state is the fiftieth state?" George asked. Then he covered his mouth quickly. He hadn't meant to talk without raising his hand. It had just happened. **And he couldn't even blame the burp.**

But Mrs. Kelly didn't seem angry. "I'm glad somebody asked that question, George," she said. "It's Hawaii. We're going to study all fifty states, starting with the newest one. After finishing your research on Hawaii, each of you is going to make a project and present it to the class."

"Can we work in groups?" Alex asked.

"You can work alone or in groups of no more than three people," Mrs. Kelly said. "But if you work in groups, I expect your project to be **extra special**."

"Want to work with me?" Alex whispered to George as the class lined up at the door. "I bet we come up with something really awesome."

"Totally," George agreed. "We'll do a project Mrs. Kelly won't ever forget."

A few minutes later, George and Alex were seated at a table in the library looking at books about Hawaii.

"We could do a report on surfing," George said. "Did you know skateboarding was started by surfers? **It's kind of like surfing on land**."

Alex shook his head. "I don't think Mrs. Kelly would like hearing about skateboarding," he reminded George. "Not so soon after what happened."

George frowned. Alex was right. It was probably best not to remind his teacher about when he skateboarded through the halls of Edith B. Sugarman Elementary School.

"So what else can we do that's cool?" George asked. "I'm not making grass skirts or flower leis."

"And I don't ever want to **hula dance** again, either," Alex said.

"Definitely not," George agreed. He turned the page in one of his books. Something caught his eye. "That's it!" he said suddenly.

"Shhh . . ." Mrs. Kelly whispered.

Oops. George lowered his voice immediately. "The book says Hawaii is built on volcanoes," he whispered to Alex. **"Let's make a volcano."**

"Cool!" Alex whispered back. "We can build it out of clay."

"And then we can make it erupt at the end of our presentation," George added.

"How can we do that?" Alex asked.

George shrugged. "I'm not sure. But I bet we can find directions for making **an erupting volcano**."

For the next forty-five minutes, Alex and George looked in books with science experiments until they found directions for making a fake volcano erupt.

"This is going to be so cool," Alex said. "We can build a little clay village around the volcano."

"Yeah, and when the lava spills out, it'll destroy all the buildings," George said excitedly. "Just knock them to the ground and **bury them in hot, flowing goo**."

"I have tons of old action figures we can use as villagers," Alex added.

At just that moment, Louie

and Max walked past the desk where
George and Alex were sitting.

"What are you two so excited about?"
Louie asked.

"Our project," Alex said. "It's going to
be **amazing**."

"What are you doing?" Louie asked.

Alex opened his mouth to answer, but
George stopped him.

"It's **a surprise**," George told Louie. "And there's a lot we need to do."

"Let's go to my house right after school," Alex suggested.

"Sounds like a plan," George said.

"Oh, no, it doesn't," Louie told George.

"Why not?" George asked.

"Because you're trying out for the band," Louie answered.

"Since when?" George asked.

"Since now," Louie told him. "Unless you don't want to be in the band. Today's the only day you can try out."

George looked from Alex to Louie and back again. He didn't know what to do.

"It's okay," Alex told George. "We can get started tomorrow after school."

"Be at my house at four," Louie said. "And **you'd better be as good as you say you are**. Because Mike and I are awesome."

"Hey, what about me?" Max asked Louie.

"Oh yeah," Louie said. "You make good peanut butter and jelly sandwiches."

"That's my job," Max said proudly. "I'm the roadie."

"I like PB&J," George told Max.

"You don't get any sandwiches unless you make the band," Louie said to George. "And I'm the one who decides if you're in or out."

Chapter 6

"Remember, I decide if you're in our band," Louie told George when he got to Louie's house.

"I know," George told him. **How could he *not* know?** Louie had been reminding him all day long. He almost felt like saying, "Forget it, find somebody else to be in your dumb band." But he didn't. That wouldn't be cool. And the whole point of being in a band was to be cool.

"Everything is set up in the basement," Louie told George. **"Keyboard, drums, and guitar amps, too."**

"You play all those instruments?" George asked.

Louie shook his head. "I just play guitar. My brother, Sam, plays drums and guitar. And my *mother* plays keyboard. Just like you."

Mike and Max thought that was **hilarious**. Max laughed so hard, he actually snorted.

George frowned. He knew why they were laughing. It was never cool to do something that someone's mother did.

"Come on, **let's get started**," Louie said as he began to lead the boys to the basement. He sped down one of the long hallways on the wheels in his sneakers.

Louie's house was huge! The dining room was big enough to fit their whole class for lunch!

No wonder Louie has sneakers with wheels, George thought. *He needs wheels to get around this place!*

As George passed the family room, he saw the walls were covered with photos. Most were of Louie and his brother on vacations—at the beach, on skis, and at amusement parks. In the living room, George spotted a **huge, flat screen TV**. Wow! It would be awesome to have one of those.

George followed Louie down the narrow stairs off the kitchen to the basement. Sure enough, there were the **drums**, the **amps**, and a small, black **keyboard**. There were also glass shelves with about a million trophies and ribbons on them.

"Are these yours?" George asked Louie.

Louie shook his head. "Uh—most of them are my brother Sam's."

"Sam's the star pitcher for the middle school baseball team," Max told George.

"And last year he won the county spelling bee," Mike added.

"I have trophies, too," Louie said. "Like over there. I got that one for coming in third in a swim race at camp."

"Cool," George said.

"And this year, I'm going to win first place in the talent show," Louie said. "You get a trophy for that. Well, don't just stand there," he said. "Let's see what you can do."

George could feel **a nervous feeling** starting up in his belly. It wasn't like bouncing burp bubbles or anything. It was more like a bunch of slimy worms crawling all around inside him.

But that wasn't going to stop George from playing. He knew he was good. Now he'd show Louie. He wriggled his fingers to loosen them up. Then he started playing one of his favorites from when he was in Slinky and the Worms.

"**Bang your head**. Stomp your feet. Don't you think music's neat?" George sang as he played the keyboard.

"What song is that?" Louie asked him.

"It's called 'Bang Your Head,'" George answered.

"I've never heard of it," Louie said.

"Me neither," Max agreed.

"That's because **I wrote it**," George said. "Well, me and my friends Kevin and Jeremy. The kids in Cherrydale really liked it."

"Well, this is Beaver Brook," Louie said. "How can I tell if you're playing all the right notes if it's **a made-up song**?"

George shrugged. "I can play something else. How about 'Don't Stop Believing'?"

"My brother's band played that in their concert last year," Louie said.

George smiled proudly. He knew that Sam was in middle school. George was only in elementary school and he already knew the song. He put his fingers on the keyboard and began to play. George didn't miss a note.

When the song ended, George waited for someone to say something. But no one did. At least not at first. Then finally, **Louie frowned.**

"I guess that was okay," he said. "And besides, we need a keyboard in the band. You're in."

"Awesome," George said. And he really meant it.

"Are you hungry?" Max asked.

George looked over at the table in the corner where Max was making sandwiches. He watched Max smear some grape jelly and peanut butter on two slices of bread. **He wiped some snot** from his nose with his hand and then slapped the slices of bread together.

"Here," Max said.

"Um . . . no thanks," George told him. "I'm not really hungry." *Anymore.*

"Okay, so now we have to come up with a name for the band," Louie said. "What do you guys think of Louie and the Lice?"

George made a face. "I don't want to be called a louse."

"Well, I like it," Louie said. "And unless you can come up with something better, that's the name."

Snort. George listened as Max sucked some snot back up his nose. Then he watched as he wiped his nose with the back of his hand.

"What about the Runny Noses," George said quietly.

"What did you say?" Louie asked him.

"The Runny Noses," George repeated. "We could be the Runny Noses."

"That's pretty good," Mike said. Then he looked quickly over at Louie. "I mean, I'm not sure. Do you like it, Louie?"

"It's actually not bad," Louie told him.

"Where'd you get that idea?" Max asked George. **"Aaachooo!"**

George laughed. "I guess it was just something I heard somewhere."

"Well, pretty soon everyone is going to hear about us," Louie said. "The Runny Noses are going to be the biggest band in **Edith B. Sugarman Elementary** history!"

"What do you mean, you don't know how to play 'Don't Drop the Rock'?" Louie shouted at George during their band rehearsal a few days later. "It's the first song you learn on guitar."

"But I don't play guitar," George told Louie. "I play piano. Do you know **'I'm Not Lazy, I'm Just Crazy'**?"

"Never heard of it," Louie said.

"Me neither," Mike said. He bashed his cymbals, and then hit one of his drums. "I want to play something with a fast beat."

"Anyone want **a salami sandwich**?" Max asked.

"No!" Mike, Louie, and George all shouted at once. It was the first thing the three of them had agreed on all afternoon.

"This is why my old band wrote our own songs," George told Louie and Mike. "That way we all learned the song together."

"Will you stop talking about your old band?" Louie shouted. Then he stopped for a minute. **"I know,"** he said. "Why don't we write our own song? Something no one has ever heard before. Then they won't know if we're playing right or wrong."

George was about to say that he'd just suggested that. But he knew Louie well enough not to bother.

An hour later, the Runny Noses had written their first song. Well, at least part of it, anyway.

"Let's take it from the top," Louie told George and Mike. "Then maybe we can figure out what's not working."

George put his fingers on the keyboard. Mike **clicked his sticks** together.

"Five, six, seven, eight . . ." Mike said.

"What are you doing?" Louie demanded.

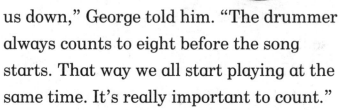

"He's counting us down," George told him. "The drummer always counts to eight before the song starts. That way we all start playing at the same time. It's really important to count."

"Then I should do it," Louie said. "After all, I'm the leader of this band."

George shrugged. He didn't really care who counted. Just as long as they could play already.

"Five, six, seven, eight," Louie counted. Then the band started to play.

"We're the Runny Noses and we're running after you . . ." Louie sang.

The guys didn't get too far into the song before **Louie's big brother**, Sam, came downstairs to see what was going on.

"Yo, dude, is this your band?" Sam asked Louie.

"Yeah," Louie said. He sounded more quiet than usual.

"I never heard that song before," Sam said.

"Yeah, well, we wrote it," Louie mumbled. **He slumped a little bit**. "I know it's not great but we're . . ."

"No, it's actually pretty good," Sam told him.

Louie stood a little taller. "I wrote most of it," he boasted.

George knew **that wasn't true**. But he didn't say anything.

"But the opening chords need some work," Sam said.

"That's just what I was thinking," Louie agreed.

"Mind if I take a crack at it?" Sam asked. "Maybe I can help you guys out."

Louie shrugged, and slipped out of his guitar strap. "Sure, if you want," he said, handing Sam the guitar.

"Cool," Sam said. He swung the guitar strap over his shoulder and looked at Mike. "**Count us down**, would you, Mike?"

"Okay," Mike said. He clicked his sticks. **"Five, six, seven, eight . . ."**

Sam began to play. He was really good. Louie was good, too. But not like his brother. Sam knew exactly which chords gave the song a really strong opening riff.

Louie sat on the couch, watching as Sam led the Runny Noses through the beginning of their new song. **There was a funny expression on his face.**

Having a brother who was amazing at everything had to be tough when you were just a normal kid. Not that anyone would *ever* accuse Louie of being normal.

Chapter 7

"Okay, this guy can go over here," Alex said. He put an action figure near the base of the volcano he and George had built. It was Saturday morning, and they were putting the finishing touches on their Hawaii project.

"You're putting R2D2 in a Hawaiian village?" George asked Alex. "He's a robot."

"But he's broken, so I don't care if he gets messed up," Alex said.

"**I guess** it will work," George said.

"Once the volcano erupts, you won't be able to see him or any of that village."

"That's kind of **a bummer**," Alex said. "We worked so hard on it this week."

George nodded. They had done lots of research on Mauna Loa, the largest volcano in the world. Building the volcano and village hadn't been easy, because Louie had called about a million band rehearsals. It had been a long week. But at least **George had been burp-free**.

"Erupting is what volcanoes do," George told Alex. "They explode and destroy. Kapow!"

"Kapow!" Alex repeated. "You're sure about how much baking soda and cherry Jell-O powder to pour into the vinegar?"

"Exactly half of this bag," George said, holding up a plastic bag filled with Jell-O powder and baking soda. "Any less and it won't explode. Any more, and we'll make a major mess."

"This is going to be so cool," Alex said. **"I can't wait until Monday morning!"**

George nodded. "When this volcano erupts, everyone is going to totally freak."

"Some leis are made from flowers. Others are made from seashells or feathers," Sage said as she gave her report to the class on Monday morning. She had

a **lei around her neck**.

"When someone gives you a lei, it is supposed to show that they like you."

George put his hand over his mouth and tried to hide a yawn. Sage's report was boring. Louie's report on ukuleles hadn't been much better.

In fact, so far, the

only report that had been
even *kind of* cool
was Julianna's
about poi. **Poi was
this soupy,
pudding-y
mush** that
was made of
the root of
some plant. Julianna had made

enough for everyone to try. And the way
you ate it was by scooping it up with your
fingers. It didn't taste bad for something
that looked pretty nasty.

George thought the poi looked a little
like the **"George soup"** he used to make
during lunchtime at his old school—
especially the kind where he mixed up
fruit punch, vanilla pudding, and salad
dressing. When he was really goofing
off, he used to stick some of his action

figures in the George soup and pretend they were stuck in quicksand. *Good times.*

Today, those same action figures were *really* going to get it. Just as soon as the volcano exploded!

Finally, it was George and Alex's turn. They carried their volcano to the front of the room. George placed it on the table and stood back. Then he reached into his pocket and pulled out the container of **secret erupting powder**. At the end of Alex's report on the **Mauna Loa volcano**, George was going to pour half of the powder into the bottle of vinegar that was hidden inside the volcano, and make it erupt.

"The Hawaiian islands were all created by volcanoes," Alex said. "They started from hot spots deep in the earth. A stream of superhot rock, called lava, was forced up from the hot spot. This caused volcanoes to form."

George stood there quietly, listening to Alex speak. Suddenly, he felt something **weird** in the bottom of his belly. It was a fizzy feeling. Like a million soda bubbles were bouncing around in there.

Oh no! Not the super burp! He'd been burp-less for a week! How could this be happening now?

"This volcano is called Mauna Loa, which means Long Mountain in Hawaiian," Alex read from his paper. "It's the largest volcano on our planet . . ."

George couldn't pay attention to what Alex was saying. He couldn't pay attention to anything but the burp swelling inside him—the super burp. It was back, and it wanted to come out. Already the bubbles were bing-bonging in George's belly, and ping-ponging their way up into his chest.

"Mauna Loa has erupted thirty-nine times since 1832," Alex continued. "Its most recent eruption was in 1984. And scientists say it is sure to erupt again . . ."

George had to stop that burp. He just had to. **He shut his lips tight and held his nose.** Then he swallowed really hard, trying to force the burp back down his throat.

But the super burp was strong. It had been kept down for too long. It needed to break free.

The biggest burp in the world erupted. **A supercolossal, Mauna Loa-size burp.** A burp so loud, it could probably be heard

all the way across the Pacific Ocean in
Hawaii!

Alex stopped talking and stared at
George. The kids all started laughing.
Mrs. Kelly stood up.

"Quiet, class," she said. "I'm sure
George didn't mean to do that."

That was sure the truth.

George opened his mouth to say,
"Excuse me." But nothing came out.
Instead, his hands started moving. It
was like they had a mind of their own.
They popped off the top of the container
they had been holding. There was no
way to stop them from pouring *all* of the
secret erupting powder into the
vinegar.

"George!" Alex shouted. "What are
you doing? You're only supposed to put in
half of the powd—"

Alex never finished his sentence.

The volcano began to shake. It began to tremor. And then . . .

KAPOW! The volcano erupted. Ruby red "lava" gel shot way up in the air!

Now George's feet wanted to have some fun. They began to leap up and down like they were on fiery coals.

"Hot! Hot!" George's mouth shouted out. **"Hot lava!"**

George began to roll on the floor under the shower of vinegar, Jell-O, and

baking soda lava. "Oh no! **I'm being buried by lava!**" he shouted.

"George! What are you doing?" Mrs. Kelly scolded. She pulled a tissue out from her sleeve, and wiped **lava splatters** from her glasses. "This is a science project, not the talent show."

But **George couldn't stop himself**. He wasn't in charge of his own body. The super burp was. And the super burp wanted George to roll around on the floor.

"Hot lava!" he shouted. "Help!"

Whoosh! Suddenly, George felt something pop in his belly. It was kind of like a balloon being punctured with a needle. All the air rushed right out of him. **The super burp was gone.**

But George was still there. In front of the classroom. On the floor. With red lava

all over the place. He opened his mouth to say, "I'm sorry." And those were exactly the words that came out.

"What were you thinking?" Mrs. Kelly asked.

She didn't sound angry. She sounded disappointed. That was worse.

George knew he'd better not say that he *wasn't* thinking. That was the kind of answer that could get a kid in even more trouble. So instead, he said, "I guess I was trying to show how sometimes volcanoes can erupt without warning. I didn't mean to mess up the classroom." **That was the truth.** He hadn't.

Mrs. Kelly sighed. "It's true that volcanoes can erupt suddenly. But I don't think what you did was the best way to demonstrate that."

"**I'm really sorry**, Mrs. Kelly," George said. He looked down at the gooey, red mess in front of him.

Mrs. Kelly looked puzzled and shook her head. "That's a start," she told him. "Shouldn't you also tell Alex you're sorry? After all, he worked hard on this project."

"I'm really sorry, dude," George said to Alex. **"I didn't mean to ruin everything."**

Alex didn't answer. George could tell he was really mad. Nothing George could say or do was going to make this better right now.

Sadly, George looked up at Mrs. Kelly. "I guess I'll go find Mr. Coleman and get a mop," he told his teacher.

"It's going to take a while to clean up this mess." Mrs. Kelly shook her head again. "I honestly don't know why you do these things, George."

George knew why. But he didn't know why the super burp picked him of all kids in the world as the victim. **It wasn't fair. Not at all.**

George skateboarded home from band rehearsal later that day. He was really lonely. Even people on the street seemed to move far away from him. Of course that was probably because they didn't want him to crash into them. Or maybe because **he smelled nasty**—like old salad dressing, from the vinegar and Jell-O that had been in his hair.

As George turned the corner and skateboarded onto his block, he spotted Chris and Alex tossing a ball around on Alex's front lawn. George could tell they

both saw him. He could also tell from
Alex's face that he didn't want anything
to do with George right now.

"Yo, George," Chris called out. "Want
to throw a ball around with us?"

George looked over at Alex. "Okay
with you?" he asked.

Alex just shrugged. **"Whatever."**

"I really am sorry about today," he
said. It was about the tenth time he'd
said it.

"You said you knew how much stuff to put in. And why didn't you wait until I was done talking?" Alex wanted to know. "That was the plan. You were supposed to surprise everyone else but not *me*."

George wanted to say that he was just as surprised as Alex. But that would sound ridiculous. So instead he just said, "It was just **something that came over me**."

Now Alex laughed. "It came over you, all right." He was looking at the big, red stains on George's T-shirt. "*All* over you."

"Oh yeah," George agreed. **"My mom's going to freak."**

Chris held up the baseball. "You want to practice some killer ball moves? Maybe we can finally beat Louie's team."

"Sure," George said. "I'll be 'it' and try to tag you with the ball." He stopped for a minute. "**I mean if that's okay** with you guys."

"It's cool," Alex said. "I'll be 'it' after you."

"And then me," Chris agreed.

"We're definitely getting better at this game," Alex said as he started to run away from the ball.

"Yeah, we are," George agreed. And now that he and Alex were talking again, he was *feeling* a lot better, too.

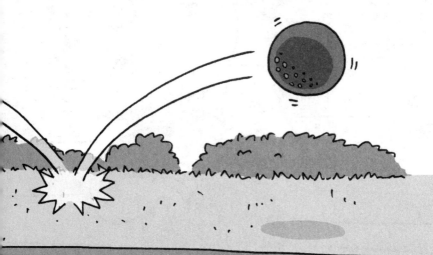

Chapter 8

For the next week, the burps only came after George left school. One came right when he was getting ready for bed, one in the storage room of his mom's craft store, and one while he was in the shower. That wasn't so bad. **At least there hadn't been any burping at school.** Which was good, because George had to spend a lot of extra time at school after classes, learning how to work the curtains in the auditorium.

George had signed up to work backstage during the talent show. He was in charge of the curtains. But when the Runny Noses went onstage, Alex was going to take over pulling the curtains. So all week long, he and Alex had spent a lot of time with Mrs. Kelly. She showed them how to work the stage lights and pull the thick cords that lifted and lowered the stage curtains between acts. It wasn't as easy as it looked. George was taking it very seriously. There was no room for joking around backstage.

"Okay, who's next?" Mrs. Kelly asked Alex, as the backstage crew got ready for the next act to go onstage on the night of the talent show.

Alex looked at his clipboard. "Chris."

"It's *my* turn already?" Chris asked. His face was ghost white. "I can't do it. **I'm too scared**."

"What do you mean?" George asked him. "You've been practicing for two weeks. And your **Toiletman** costume looks great. Your mom even bought you a new plunger!"

"What if nobody likes my jokes?" Chris said.

"They'll like them," George told him.

"Toiletman's funny," Alex agreed.

"But you guys are my friends," Chris said. "There are **a whole bunch of people** out there I don't know."

George thought for a minute. Then he said, "They're people just like us. They put their **underwear** on one leg at a time."

Chris stared at him.

"My dad said something like that to my mom when she had to make a speech to the PTA in my old school," George explained. "The point is, if you picture the people in the **audience in their underwear**, they won't seem so scary."

Chris started to laugh.

"What's so funny?" Alex asked him.

"I'm picturing Mr. Trainer in **tighty-whities**," Chris said.

Mr. Trainer was their gym teacher.

"See?" George told Chris. "It's working already."

Chris picked up his **toilet seat shield**, **his plunger**, **his toilet brush**, and a roll of toilet paper. "Toiletman will not be flushed," he said. "The show must go on."

George began to open the curtains. **"Go, Toiletman.** I know you'll *bowl* them over!"

Once the clapping for Chris stopped, George brought down the curtains. It was time for Sage and her friends to do their dance. The girls were all dressed in different colored leotards and tights. They were each supposed to be one of the four seasons.

Up went the curtain again. George watched the girls wave their arms around and leap across the floor. **It was boring,** but watching was part of a curtain guy's job. As soon as the dance was over, he had to pull on the ropes and close the curtains.

So George watched as Sage jumped up high in her autumn costume, and bashed Ariella in the nose. Nobody stopped dancing even though **Ariella's nose was bleeding all over the place**. Wow. This was getting to be sort of entertaining, after all.

Then, right in the middle of the bloody ballet, George suddenly felt something weird happening in the bottom of his belly. There was a bubble in there. **A *big* bubble.** And it was starting to jump around.

Oh no! Not the super burp. ***Not now.***

The bubbles were already **ping-ponging** around in his stomach and threatening to move up into his chest. George gulped. **This couldn't happen.** Not in the middle of the talent show. There was no telling what his hands and feet would do if they got control of the curtains. Or worse, what if the super burp made him go out there and leap around with Sage and her friends?!

George had to **beat the burp!** Quickly, he shoved his whole fist in his mouth. There was no way the burp was getting past *that*!

But the burp was strong. And it was determined. It kept bouncing and bouncing around. George used his free hand to pound his stomach, trying to pop that bubble from the outside.

At just that moment, Louie, Max, and Mike walked over.

"Yo, what is the matter with you?" Louie asked him.

George didn't answer. He couldn't. He had his fist shoved in his mouth.

Then, suddenly, George felt something go **pop** inside. *Whoosh!* It felt like all the air rushed right out of him. **Yahoo! George had done it!** He'd squelched the belch!

George took his hand out of his mouth. He wiped his wet, **spit-covered** fingers on his jeans.

"Why were you sucking on your fingers?" Louie asked. "It's gross."

"*Really* gross," Max agreed.

"Um, it's called **a vocal exercise**," George said quickly. "You have to try and sing through your hand, while tapping on your belly." There. That sounded believable. Sort of.

"Yeah, well, don't do it again," Louie said. "You look **weird**. And I don't want anyone thinking the Runny Noses are weird."

"No problem," George said.

Just then, Alex came running over. He grabbed hold of the ropes and began lowering the curtains as Sage and her friends ran offstage. It was his turn to be the curtain guy.

"Are you guys ready?" Alex asked the Runny Noses.

George sure hoped so.

Chapter 9

"We're the Runny Noses, and we're running after you. We're the Runny Noses, can't be stopped with no tissue . . ."

George sang the background vocals as he played his keyboard. He looked into the audience to see if he could spot his parents. There were a lot of people out there, but it was *always* easy to find his dad. An army uniform really stood out in a crowd.

"Coming to you as hard as a sneeze. We'll play just as long as we please . . ."

The lyrics were **pretty dumb**. Louie had written them, and Mike and Max kept saying how cool the song was. So those were the words they used.

George tried to play in time with Mike's drums. **It wasn't easy.** Every now and then, Mike would speed up or slow down. But then again, George didn't always play the right notes. And Louie had forgotten a couple of words in the first verse. But no one seemed to notice. In fact, some people were clapping along.

George was starting to have a good time. Then, **suddenly**, he got a strange feeling in his stomach. A bunch of bubbles were suddenly bouncing up and down and all around in his belly.

Oh no! Not again!

George had to stop that burp right now! But this time he couldn't use his hands to beat down the burp. He had to keep playing.

So he just held his breath until his face
turned red.

Louie turned around to face George.
"What are you doing?" he whispered
angrily.

George didn't answer. He couldn't.

The bubbles ping-pong-pinged their
way up out of George's stomach.

They **boing-bing-boinged** their way to
his chest.

They bing-boing-binged their way up
his throat. And then . . .

George let out the loudest burp
in the history of Edith B. Sugarman
Elementary School. In fact, if burping
counted as a talent, George would have

walked away with a trophy. The super-duper **mega-burping trophy**!

The audience laughed really hard. Louie and Mike just stared at him.

"It wasn't me," George said.

The words slipped right out of George's mouth. He hadn't meant to say them.

The audience just laughed harder.

And then George's feet got a great idea! They slipped right out of their shoes and **wriggled out of his socks**. Then his feet propped themselves up on the keyboard.

George tried to stop them. He tried to slap them down from the piano.

"Stop!" he ordered.

But George's feet would not obey. His toes wanted to play the keyboard. *Go tell Aunt Rhodie. Go tell Aunt Rhodie . . .*

"What are you playing?" Louie asked. **"That's for kindergartners!"**

But it was the only song George's toes knew. So they kept playing it.

Go tell Aunt Rhodie. Go tell Aunt Rhodie . . . Go tell Aunt Rhodie, the old gray goose is dead.

"Cut it out!" Louie shouted.

George turned and smiled at the audience. He stood up and took a bow. **The kids all cheered wildly.**

And then, before George even knew what he was doing . . .

"Dive-bomb!" George shouted as he took a flying leap off the stage.

Wahoo! George was soaring in the air, and heading right for the crowd.

A bunch of older kids—one of them was Louie's brother—reached up. Two kids caught his legs. Someone's dad caught him right in the armpits. His head fell into someone's arms.

The crowd cheered wildly. **"George! George! George!"**

Pop! Just then, George felt something burst in his belly. *Whoosh.* All the air rushed right out of him.

The super burp was gone. But George was still there. As he looked up, he realized Mrs. McKeon was holding his head. And she did not look happy.

Uh-oh. George had just **dive-bombed into the principal**. This was *ba-a-ad!*

Chapter 10

"**I can't believe** we didn't even come in third," Mike complained as he packed up his drumsticks after the talent show.

"Are you kidding?" Louie asked. "After what he did, we're lucky we didn't get thrown out of school."

George looked down at the ground. He felt **really bad**. Louie had wanted a trophy. They all did. And maybe they would have gotten one, except for the stupid super burp.

"We never should have let you in the band," Louie told George. **"You messed the whole thing up.** If I was Mrs. McKeon, I'd take away your recess for a whole year."

George couldn't imagine what Louie would be like as principal of a school. It was **too scary** to think about.

"You're going to be sorry you did this to me . . . I mean to *us*," Louie said. **"You're out of the band!"**

Just then, Sam and two other middle-school kids came backstage.

They were heading toward the band. *Uh-oh.* The last thing George wanted now was some older kids making fun of him.

Louie looked kind of nervous as his brother walked closer and closer. "You guys were good!" Sam said.

"Really, Sam? You really thought—" Louie said.

Sam didn't answer. Instead he was looking at George. "And you! You were **amazing, dude**," he told George.

"Playing keyboard with your toes!" Sam's friend added. "How do you do that?"

"The **dive-bomb** was the best part," Sam said.

"You guys were ripped off," the third middle-schooler told them. "You should have won."

George just stood there, surprised. He wasn't sure what to say.

"That dive-bomb was my idea," Louie told Sam. "I would have done it myself, but I didn't want to break my guitar."

George shook his head. Louie was **unbelievable**.

"At our next concert, *I'm* going to

dive-bomb," Louie told George.

Huh? **Their next concert?** What next
concert? Hadn't Louie just thrown him
out of the band?

Just then, Alex came over. "My mom
said you and your parents should come
for ice cream with us," he said to George.
"We're going to Ernie's Ice Cream
Emporium."

Ernie's. That was the last place George wanted to go tonight. That was where it had all started. It was the **scene of the first burp**. And George had had enough burping for one night.

"I better not," George told Alex. "My parents will be waiting for me out in the hall. I have a feeling they're not going to want me to go anywhere. They're probably going to want to *talk*."

Alex nodded and then shook his head sadly. When parents wanted to talk, **it was never a good thing**.

"Well, let's hang out tomorrow if you're allowed," Alex told him. **"I'm still working on how to ollie."**

Louie shook his head. "George can't skateboard tomorrow. He's got band practice."

"Sorry, Louie. **It's not happening**," George told him. "I'm hanging out with

Alex tomorrow."

Louie stared at George, like he couldn't believe anyone would turn down a chance to hang out with him.

"We can rehearse on Sunday, though," George said.

Louie didn't look happy. But all he said was, "Okay, Sunday. Cool."

Suddenly, George heard a loud, grumbly, rumbly noise. It was coming from his stomach!

Everyone just stopped and stared.

"Dude, gross," the fifth-grader said.

A familiar feeling came over George. He put his hand on his stomach. And then . . . he smiled. There was no burp in there. In fact there was *nothing* in there. His stomach was just empty.

"I'm **starving**. My stomach always grumbles when I'm hungry," George explained.

George was **happy to be burp-free**—
at least for now. But somehow he had a
feeling the super burp would be back.
He just didn't know when. Or what it
would make him do. The only thing he
knew for sure was that when that burp
came back, it was going to cause trouble.
And that was just plain *ba-a-ad*!

George Brown, CLASS CLOWN

World's Worst Wedgie

by Nancy Krulik

illustrated by Aaron Blecha

Grosset & Dunlap

An Imprint of Penguin Group (USA) Inc.

Chapter 1

"Check this out, you guys!"

George Brown took off down the block on his skateboard. It popped up and spun around in midair before George landed on it and rolled down the street.

George smiled. **Now *that* was some serious liftoff!**

"Whoa!" George's friend Alex cheered. "When did you learn that?"

"Yesterday," George said. "At Tyler's Toy Shop."

"They give skateboarding lessons there?" George's other friend Chris asked.

"No," George said. "But they had this really cool remote-controlled toy called **Dude-on-a-Skateboard**. I played with it and this was one of the tricks you could make it do. Then I practiced doing it myself later."

"So will your parents buy it for you?" Chris asked.

George shook his head. "Forget it. It was

fifteen dollars. They said if I want it so badly, I can save up my allowance."

Alex shrugged. "I guess you're not getting it anytime soon."

"What's that supposed to mean?" George asked.

"Nothing," Alex said. "It's just that you're lousy at saving money."

"Yeah," Chris agreed. "Remember that time you went to the comic book store with me? You bought three comics, ones you don't even like."

"Or the last time we went to the penny candy store?" Alex asked. "You blew three dollars there. No one can eat three hundred pieces of penny candy. But you had three bucks, so you spent three bucks."

George didn't answer Chris or Alex. What could he say? They were right. George *was* a lousy saver.

George rode the rest of the way to school on his skateboard while Chris and Alex walked behind him. When they reached the school yard, they saw a big crowd of fourth-graders gathered by one of the big oak trees.

"What's going on?" Chris asked.

George skateboarded over to find out.

Louie was standing in the middle of the group—with a remote control in his hands. George looked down and watched the Dude-on-a-Skateboard spin around in a perfect 360. **How come Louie was always the first one to get anything cool?**

"Check it out!" Louie told the kids. "I can make my RC Dude-on-a-Skateboard **pop a wheelie!**"

"Pretty cool!" Julianna said.

"Can I try?" George asked.

"Why should I let you?" Louie asked.

"Umm, because it's nice to share?" George suggested.

"I *am* sharing," Louie told him.

"*How* are you sharing?" George asked.

"I'm letting you watch," Louie told him.

"See?" Max said, turning to George. "He told you he was sharing."

George frowned. He started to say how sharing had a whole different meaning in Louie's world. But he stopped mid-sentence and shut his mouth tight.

Louie didn't seem to notice. He was too busy flicking the switch on his remote. All the kids were watching the Dude-on-a-Skateboard whirl around in circles.

All except George. He couldn't watch.
He was too freaked out by the bubbles that
had suddenly started bouncing around
in his belly. **There was a burp brewing in
there.** And not just any burp. From the
way those bubbles were bing-bonging
around, George could tell this was a *super
burp*. **It wanted out**, but there was no way
George was going to let *that* happen!

All of a sudden, he began to spin around
and around in circles. He wanted to force

that burp to swirl its way back down to his toes—just the way water swirls its way back down the toilet after you flush.

"Yo! Check out George!" Alex said. The kids all turned to watch George spin around and around in circles.

"Hey!" Louie shouted. "Are you making fun of my Dude-on-a-Skateboard?"

George wasn't making fun of anything. He was just trying to **squelch a belch**. But he couldn't tell Louie that. The super burp was George's secret. And he was going to keep it that way.

Chapter 2

It had all started on George's first day at Edith B. Sugarman Elementary School. George's family had moved—again. That meant George was the new kid—again. George's dad was in the army, so his family moved around a lot.

This time, George had promised himself that he was **turning over a new leaf**. No more pranks. No more class clown. He wasn't going to get into any trouble anymore, like he had at all his old schools.

At first, it really worked. George raised his hand before answering questions. He didn't make faces or laugh behind teachers' backs.

But George didn't have to be a math whiz like his pal Alex to figure out how many friends being a new, well-behaved kid would get him. The answer was easy. **Zero. Nada. Zilch.**

That night, George's parents took him out to Ernie's Ice Cream Emporium. While they were sitting outside and George was finishing his root beer float, a shooting star flashed across the sky. So George made a wish.

I want to make kids laugh—but not get into trouble.

Unfortunately, the star was gone before George could finish the wish. So only half came true—**the first half**.

A minute later, George had a funny feeling in his belly. It was like there were hundreds of tiny bubbles bouncing around in there. The bubbles ping-ponged their way into his chest and bing-bonged their way up into his throat. And then . . .

George let out a big burp. A *huge* burp. A SUPER burp!

The super burp was loud, and it was *magical*.

Suddenly George lost control of his arms and legs. It was like they had minds of their own. His hands grabbed straws and stuck them up his nose like a walrus. His feet jumped up on the table and started dancing. **Everyone at Ernie's started laughing**— except George's parents, who were covered in ice cream from the sundaes he had knocked over.

That wasn't the only time the super burp had burst its way out of George's belly. George never knew when a burp would strike or what it would make him do. Like juggle raw eggs in his classroom (which would have been fine if George actually knew *how* to

juggle) or make his model volcano erupt in red goo all over his teacher or dive-bomb the audience during a talent show.

Every time the burp came, George made the other kids laugh. But he also managed to make grown-ups **really mad**.

That was why George was determined to keep this burp from bursting out. He didn't know what he might do if it exploded out of him. But he did know where he would wind up: **in trouble**. *And* in the principal's office.

So George kept spinning

and spinning, trying to force that burp down the drain.

Whoosh. Suddenly George felt a huge bubble pop inside his stomach. All the air rushed right out of him. The fizzy feeling was gone.

All right! **George had beaten the burp!** He stopped spinning and pumped his fist in the air.

"What was that all about?" Louie asked.

George had to say something—fast!

"It's your fault," George told Louie. "You were making me spin."

"Huh?" Louie asked.

"It's that remote control," George said. "It's sending signals to the metal filling in my tooth. It's making me spin, see?"

The kids all started laughing.

"Hey, it's making me spin, too," Chris added. He began whirling around and around.

A minute later all the kids were spinning in circles. Well, **almost** all of them, anyway. Max

and Mike stopped spinning after Louie shot them dirty looks.

"You are **so weird**," Louie told George.

George shrugged. He didn't mind Louie calling him weird. It was better than Louie calling him crazy. And crazy was definitely what Louie would think if George ever told him about the super burp.

Chapter 3

"George, can you tell us the name of the capital of Alaska?"

Uh-oh. Mrs. Kelly had caught him doodling in his notebook. The old George hardly ever paid attention in class. But **the new George didn't daydream**. At least not too often.

"Um . . . I . . . ," George mumbled.

A few of the kids started to giggle.

Mrs. Kelly gave George a gummy smile. George wasn't used to having teachers like him, but for some reason, Mrs. Kelly did. "It's okay," she said. "We all have days when we are a little foggy. And *you know* a lot about geography." Mrs. Kelly said the words "you know" really loud.

Huh? If he knew a lot, he would know the capital. **Wait a minute.** Maybe Mrs. Kelly was giving him a hint.

"*You know* Alaska's capital, George. I'm sure *you know* it."

George tried to figure out what Mrs. Kelly was telling him. Then it hit him. **You know—*Juneau*!**

"The capital of Alaska is Juneau," George shouted out.

Mrs. Kelly nodded and gave George another gummy smile. "Exactly. Juneau, Alaska."

"Class, let me show you some pictures of my trip to Alaska," Mrs. Kelly said as she clicked the mouse on her computer. A picture of Mrs. Kelly in front of a totem pole appeared on the screen in the front of the room. "Here I am in a national park in Sitka, Alaska."

The face that was carved in the totem pole right above Mrs. Kelly's head had **big, buggy eyes** and a **funny, toothy frown**. It was exactly the upside down of Mrs. Kelly's big, toothy smile. George poked Alex, who sat next to him, and started to make the totem pole face. But then he stopped . . . that was *so* old George.

"And here I am on an iceberg," Mrs. Kelly said, changing the picture. "I had to fly there in a helicopter."

There was Mrs. Kelly, standing on a white block of ice.

Mrs. Kelly clicked the computer mouse again. Up came another picture of Mrs. Kelly on the iceberg. This time she was lying on the ice, with one leg in front of her, and one to the side. Her glasses were all crooked.

Mrs. Kelly quickly clicked the mouse. "Um . . . **the iceberg was really slippery**," she explained.

George made sure not to look at Alex.
If he did, he knew he'd burst out laughing.

"Here I am beating a real Alaskan drum,"
Mrs. Kelly said. "And for a special treat, I've
brought the drum in to show you."

Mrs. Kelly held up a big drum. The head
of the drum was the size of a **pizza**. A picture
of a red and blue bird with a big beak was
painted on it.

George sure hoped Mrs. Kelly wasn't going to do something weird like start banging on that drum or anything. If she did, it would be *impossible* for him not to laugh.

Before George could even finish his thought, Mrs. Kelly began banging the drum, and chanting some Native American song she'd learned from the Tlingit tribe in Alaska.

"Dei yin d'tawn," his teacher sang. "Xaan woo jee xee na."

The song was probably really cool when it was sung by someone who knew how it was supposed to go. **But Mrs. Kelly couldn't sing.** She couldn't drum very well, either.

"Hee hee yaaa," Mrs. Kelly screeched at the top of her lungs. "Hee hee yaw aanna."

George picked up his pencil and started to draw another Dude-on-a-Skateboard in his notebook. **It was the only way to stop himself from laughing at Mrs. Kelly.**

George twirled his pencil and started thinking. He got two dollars a week for his allowance. If he saved every penny, in eight weeks, he'd have more than enough money for the Dude-on-a-Skateboard.

Suddenly, George realized something important. It had nothing to do with totem poles, icebergs, or drums, though. He didn't have to wait weeks and save up. George was going to make that money, and make it **fast**.

George Brown was a man with a plan!

Chapter 4

"Mom!" George shouted on his way into the Knit Wit.

George's mom's store was a really boring place. It was full of crafty stuff like yarn, cloth, glitter, and silk flowers.

There was usually a bunch of ladies sitting around with knitting needles saying stuff like "knit one . . . purl two." Every now and then, one of them would threaten to knit a hat with a pom-pom for George because he was "just so darn cute."

He was ready to put his plan into action! "Mom!" George yelled again.

George's mother came racing out of the stock room. "What's the matter?"

"Nothing," George said. "I just wanted to talk to you."

"So talk. I'm all ears," his mom said.

"Do you need any help around here?" George said.

George's mom gave him a curious look. "You want to help me . . . *here*?"

George understood why his mom sounded so surprised. "Yeah," he said. "I thought you could give me a job."

"Why do you need a job?" George's mom asked.

"Well, I want that remote-controlled skateboard, and you said I had to pay for it. So . . ." George let his voice trail off.

"I don't know, George," his mom said.

George cocked his head to the side, and flashed his mom **a goofy, crooked smile**.

"Oh no, not your special face," his mom said.

George smiled harder. Oh *yes*. His mom could never refuse George anything when he made his **special face**.

George's mom laughed. "All right. I guess it won't do any harm to have you straighten up the shelves. And I could use someone to sort the beads. The trays are a mess."

"I'm great at cleaning up messes," George said.

"Since when?" his mom teased.

"Since right now," George promised.

A few minutes later, George was busy in the back of the store straightening up. **It was a pretty boring job.** But George didn't complain. His mom was paying him five dollars an hour. That meant all he had to do was hang in there for three hours and that RC Dude-on-a-Skateboard would be **all his**.

COTTON THREAD YARN

Once George had everything stacked up, he headed toward the bead department. And that's when he felt the bubbles—*big* bubbles. And they were all bouncing around in his belly. **Uh-oh!** Those bubbles could only mean one thing. **The super burp!**

Oh man! Not again. Two times in one day! That just wasn't fair.

George held his nose and clamped his mouth shut. Then he started jumping up and down, trying to force the bubbles down.

A little girl pointed to George. "Why is that boy acting so silly, Mommy?" she asked.

George had already kept one burp inside

today. But this one seemed determined to get out.

The bubbles ping-pong-pinged their way up out of George's stomach.

They boing-bing-boinged their way to his chest.

They bing-boing-binged their way up his throat. And then . . .

George let out a humongous burp! **The kind of burp that could be heard all the way in Juneau, Alaska.**

"George!" his mother scolded.

George opened his mouth to say, "Excuse me." But that's not what came out. Instead, George let out a loud, angry, monsterlike sound. He didn't mean to.

But George wasn't in control. The super burp had taken over. His arms and legs were on their own. His hands grabbed a big roll of pink and purple, polka-dotted cloth. His body began to spin around and around, getting all wrapped up in the material.

George's arms stuck themselves straight out and his legs began walking stiffly around the store **like a mummy in a scary movie**.

"I want my mummy!" George's mouth shouted.

"George! Stop that this minute!" his mother shouted.

But George didn't stop. He couldn't. **The super burp was in charge now.**

"That boy is funny, Mommy," the little girl by the silk flowers said.

Her sister started laughing, too.

"George!" George's mom didn't think he was funny. Not one bit.

George's body turned itself around.

His hands found a big tray of beads. They tilted the tray and . . .

Ping! Ping! Ping! Hundreds of small black and silver beads fell all over the floor.

Whoops! George's feet slid over the beads.

Wham! George's rear end bashed onto the floor. *Ow!* That one hurt.

"Arrooo!" George shouted. He sounded like a mummy in pain.

CRASH!

Whoosh. Suddenly, George felt something go pop in his stomach like someone had punctured a balloon. All the air rushed out of him. The super burp was gone!

But George was still lying there on the floor. He wasn't a mummy anymore. He was just a kid, wrapped up in a pink and purple, polka-dotted cloth. And he was in **big trouble**.

"George, look at this mess!" his mother demanded. "What got into you?"

George didn't know what to say. The problem wasn't what had gotten *into* him. It was what had slipped **out of him**. But he couldn't tell his mother about the super burp. She wouldn't believe him. She'd just think he was making a crazy excuse for his behavior. So he just opened his mouth and said, "I'm sorry. I'll clean up everything."

"You bet you will," his mother told him. "And then you'll go straight home."

"Home?" George asked. "But what about my job?"

"You don't have a job anymore," his mom said.

George couldn't believe his ears. He'd just been **fired** by his own mother. That wasn't fair. It was the stupid super burp that deserved to be fired and sent packing— anywhere. To any other kid. Because **George Brown was *sick* of burping**.

Chapter 5

"How much have you saved up?" Chris asked the next morning before school.

George felt one lonely **quarter** in his pocket. "Not much, I passed an ice cream truck yesterday."

"You bought an ice cream with the allowance money you were supposed to be saving?" Alex shook his head.

George needed ice cream after leaving his mom's store but no way was he going

into the
whole
polka-dotted
mummy
thing. So he
just said, "It
was one of
those ice creams that
looked like a cat. It had red
bubble gum eyeballs."

"I love those," Chris said.

"Me too," Alex agreed.
"But that doesn't help George
get an RC toy."

They watched Louie in the school
yard. He'd brought **Dude** with him again.

"He's just showing off," George said.

"He's charging kids a nickel to play
with it," Alex said.

"Hey! What if we pooled our money?"
George suggested. "Then we could get an

RC Dude-on-a-Skateboard and share it. Really share it. **Not *Louie*-share it**."

"That would be awesome," Chris said. "Except for one thing."

"What's that?" George asked.

"I have exactly a nickel," Chris answered.

"I only have eleven cents," Alex said. "But I borrowed a dollar from my mom last week. So that means counting all three of us, **we really have minus fifty-nine cents**."

It was pretty impressive how Alex could do math problems in his head. But having minus fifty-nine cents was **definitely not**.

"Maybe we could earn the money selling stuff," Chris suggested.

"Like what?" Alex asked. "Your comic books?"

"No way!" Chris said. "What about a lemonade stand?"

"So many kids have lemonade stands," Alex said.

"Listen," George told his friends, "my mom is always making gourmet stuff from cookbooks. Gourmet means it's better than plain old food. We're not going to sell ordinary lemonade at our stand . . . we're going to sell **gourmet lemonade**!"

"I'm worried because we didn't put in enough sugar," Alex told George. It was Saturday afternoon. The boys were lugging all the stuff for their lemonade stand to the playground.

"We used up all the sugar my mom had," George reminded him. "Anyway, remember, this is gourmet lemonade. It's not **supposed** to taste like plain old lemonade."

"I put in extra lemon juice to make up for the missing sugar," Chris said.

"Exactly," George said. "The more lemons the better. It's called lemonade. Not **sugarade**."

Alex found a shady spot beneath a tree, and Chris helped him open up the card table they'd borrowed from Alex's house.

George taped their sign to the table. It said: **"Gourmet" Lemonade! Only 10¢ A Cup!** Then he put the pitcher of lemonade and a stack of paper cups on the table.

"We're only charging **ten cents a cup**?" Alex said. "Do you guys know how long it will take us to earn fifteen dollars?"

"Kids don't have a lot of money," George told Alex. "We can't charge more."

"That's true," Alex admitted.

"Now let's get us some customers,"

George said. He reached into his backpack and pulled out a long, yellow sweatshirt and a yellow baseball hat with long plastic straws coming out of it. "One of you guys put these on."

Alex and Chris stared at him.

"GOURMET" LEMONADE! ONLY 10¢ A CUP!

"What?" they asked at the exact same time.

"This is how we advertise our gourmet lemonade," George explained.

"By putting on a hat?" Chris asked.

"It's not a hat," George told him. "It's part of **a lemonade costume**. One of you is going to dress up like a glass of lemonade and dance around."

"Why don't *you* wear it?" Alex suggested.

"Fine," George huffed. "I'll be the glass of lemonade." He slipped on the sweatshirt and the big, lemon yellow baseball hat with the giant straws hanging out of it. Then he began to **dance and sing**.

"When you're hot and really thirsty, lemonade's what you think of firsty . . ."

"Okay!" Alex shouted. "Get your gourmet lemonade! Cold, fresh lemonade!"

A few minutes later, Julianna and Sage
rode by on their bikes.

Julianna looked at George and laughed.
"Are you supposed to be a banana?"

"No," George said. "It's a lemonade
costume to advertise our lemonade stand.
Why would I be dressed as a banana?"

"I think you make a cute lemon,
Georgie," Sage said.

George ignored Sage. He didn't like her calling him **cute**.

"We're trying to raise money to buy an RC Dude-on-a-Skateboard," Chris told the girls.

"We would let you play with ours for free," George said. "Want to buy some lemonade and help us out?"

"Okay." Julianna pulled a dime out of her pocket.

"Me too," Sage said. "I want to help you get your Dude, Georgie."

George poured the lemonade. **A customer was a customer.** Even if that customer was Sage.

"Whoa!" Julianna exclaimed after her first sip. "This is **sour**."

"It's *lemon*ade," Chris said. "Lemons are sour."

Sage took a sip. She made a face. "Wow. It's definitely lemony," she said.

Then she forced a smile and looked at George. "But in a good way," she added.

"Didn't you put any sugar in?" Julianna asked him.

"Some," Chris said. "But we didn't . . ."

George nudged Chris in the ribs. "We didn't want to overpower the natural taste of the lemons," George said. "This is a **gourmet citrus beverage**."

Just then Louie, Max, and Mike showed up. Louie was holding a big, rubber ball.

"Bet you guys were playing killer ball." George said.

Louie nodded. Killer ball was a game Louie had made up. It was sort of like dodgeball, but **meaner**.

"You look like you need some lemonade," Alex told Mike and Max. "Playing killer ball can really make you thirsty."

Mike nodded. "And **black and blue**," he said.

Then he looked at Louie. "Not that I'm complaining," he added. "That's part of the game."

"What? Are you **a banana or something**?" Louie looked at George.

"No. I'm a lem—Oh, never mind," George said.

"This is gourmet lemonade," Sage told Louie.

"Yeah?" Louie asked. He plunked two dimes on the table. "Well, if it's that good, better make mine a double."

"GOURMET"
LEMONADE!

"Okay!" George said. He poured four glasses all the way to the top of the cup.

Max took a long sip of his lemonade. His lips pursed and he sucked in his cheeks. "Whoa!"

Mike tried his. He shut his eyes tight and shivered. **It looked like he had just swallowed medicine.** "It doesn't have enough sugar," he said.

Louie looked down at his cup. "I want my money back," he said.

Just then, three more kids came by.

They looked thirsty. So George ignored Louie and smiled.

But before George could say "Get your gourmet lemonade," a funny, bubbly feeling started up in his belly.

Oh no! The burp was back!

George wanted to beat the burp. He shut his mouth tight and pinched his nose.

"What are you doing?" Louie asked him.

George didn't answer. He *couldn't* answer. If he did, the burp would escape.

But this burp wasn't going to be kept down. It **bing-bonged** its way out of George's stomach and into his chest. Then it **ping-ponged** its way up into his throat. And then . . .

George let out a **superduper megahumongous** burp! A burp so strong, it knocked the yellow baseball cap right off his head.

"Whoa!" Chris shouted. "That was major."

George's hands grabbed the glass out of Max's hands and poured the super-sour lemonade down George's throat.

Suddenly George's eyes got big and buggy. Then his hands reached up and grabbed his neck.

"Aahhh . . . I've been **poisoned**!" George shouted.

His feet began stumbling all around. His eyes crossed themselves.

"Cut it out! You're going to ruin our lemonade business," Alex said.

George knew that. And he wanted to stop but unfortunately, his body had a mind of its own. And it wanted to goof around some more.

"Gak . . . ," George said. His tongue popped out. "Good-bye, cruel world." He **plopped** down on the ground, and **wiggled** all around like a crazed snake.

Max and Mike started laughing. At least they did until Louie shot them a look.

And then . . .

Whoosh. George felt something pop in his belly. It was like the air had just rushed out of him. The super burp was **gone**!

"This kid's funny," one of the boys said.

"Yeah," his friend agreed. "But I'm not touching that lemonade."

"I'm out of here," the third kid agreed.

Louie, Max, and Mike weren't far behind. Pretty soon it was just George, Alex, Chris, Sage, and Julianna at the lemonade stand.

"George, are you sure you want to buy that Dude-on-a-Skateboard?" Alex asked him.

"Because it sure seems like you were trying to wreck the whole thing," Chris added. He sounded kind of **mad**.

George hadn't tried to wreck anything. The super burp had done that. But he knew there was no way he could tell his friends that. So he just mumbled, "I'm sorry."

Stupid super burp. **Now the whole plan had gone sour.**

Chapter 6

Monday morning in the school yard, Julianna came running over to George. She was bouncing a basketball in front of her as she ran.

"Think fast!" Julianna shouted. She threw the ball at George.

Oomph. The ball hit George right in the belly. He opened his mouth slightly, and . . . belch. A burp came flying out. **Not a big burp**. But a burp just the same.

George stood there for a minute. He waited for the magic to take over. But it didn't. *Phew.* That hadn't been a super burp. It was just a **nice, normal** burp.

"Hey, that reminds me," George said. "Did you guys ever hear the joke about the burp?"

"No," Alex said.

"Never mind," George said. "It's not worth repeating." He smiled. That had been a pretty funny joke. The kind of joke **a regular kid** would tell. Not a super burp kind of joke.

"You crack me up, George," Chris said.

Alex nodded. "Too bad you can't make money **clowning around**."

George stopped for a minute and stared at his pal. "Alex! You're a genius!" he shouted.

"I know how we can make a pile of money!" George paused. "It'll mean a lot of work."

"If I help you, can I share the Dude-on-a-Skateboard with you?" Julianna asked.

"Sure," George promised her.

"You'll be a **twenty-five percent owner**," Alex said.

"Okay. I'm in," Julianna said.

"So what's the plan?" Chris asked.

Out of the corner of his eye, George spotted Louie coming up the block to school with Mike and Max. The last thing George wanted was for Louie to hear his new plan. He'd find some way to ruin it.

"I'll tell you guys later," he said. "But I promise you're going to love this idea. It's my very best one yet!"

Chapter 7

By Saturday morning, George was completely convinced that his idea—a fabulous **one-ring backyard circus**—was his greatest money-making plan ever. Right then lots of little kids were arriving at Chris's backyard with their parents. And every one of them had bought a ticket!

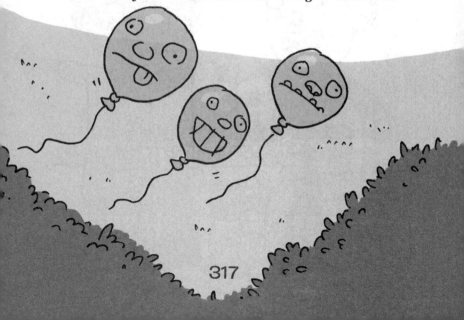

The boys and Julianna had worked hard all week selling tickets and rehearsing their acts. George couldn't wait to perform his clown act for the kids. He was going to ride around on a tricycle and tell a bunch of jokes.

"I look like an idiot," Alex groaned as he stood in the middle of the garage putting on his costume. "This is **way too small**."

"That's because it's my sister's

Halloween costume from two years ago," Chris explained.

"Don't worry," George told Alex. "Chris looks like an idiot, too."

Chris was wearing **a tiger costume** that had a headband with ears. He looked in the mirror nailed to a wall and started painting whiskers on his face. "It was the only other animal costume we had."

"Quit complaining. We've already sold twenty tickets," George told his friends. "And I bet we sell lots of refreshments."

George could see Sage setting up the refreshment stand. They'd only let Sage help because she promised to bake a lot of cookies for free. Chris's mom had baked a **Boston cream pie**. The bottom of the pie was chocolate goo and on top of that was a mountain of whipped cream. It looked so good, George thought he'd buy a slice for himself after the show.

"Okay, okay." Alex sucked in his stomach really hard and pulled on the zipper until it closed. "I just want to know why Chris gets to be a tiger and I have to be a pig. When do you ever see a pig at a circus?"

"I told you before, you're not a pig. You're a **wild boar**," George told Alex. "Wild boars are fierce! Anyway, by noon, we'll be rich."

"We all look like idiots," Alex insisted.

George looked down at his clown costume. He was wearing a red wig, his mom's polka-dot shirt, and his dad's plaid golf pants. His red clown nose itched, and his dad's sneakers were like a **trillion** sizes too big.

Just then, Julianna arrived. She was wearing a top hat, a red shirt, and black pants tucked into horseback riding boots. She really did look like **a wild animal trainer**.

Julianna stared at Alex strangely. "You're a pig? I thought you were going to be a lion. Pigs aren't circus animals."

"We couldn't find the lion costume," Chris explained.

"And he's not a pig. He's a wild boar," George told her.

George took a peek outside and

smiled. Two rows of chairs were arranged in a big circle in the backyard and every seat was filled. It was a **sold-out show**!

"Looks like it's showtime!" George said.

George stepped into the middle of the circle—the center ring. "Ladies and gentlemen. Boys and girls," he shouted in his best circus voice. "Welcome to the Big Top. We have a great show for you today. First up: wild animal trainer Julianna and her ferocious beasts!"

Julianna ran into the center ring. Chris and Alex crawled behind her on all fours.

"Oh, Georgie," someone said suddenly. "Hi there."

George turned and saw Sage. She was wearing a bright green tutu and some green feathers in her hair. Sage was going to perform tricks on the trampoline in the backyard.

George hated it when Sage called him Georgie. The way she said it made it sound like she liked him or something. **George definitely didn't like being liked by Sage.**

"You're supposed to be at the refreshment stand," George said.

She smiled. "You look cute in that costume."

"I'm not supposed to be **cute**," George

said. "I'm supposed to be **funny**."

"Oh, you're funny, too, Georgie," she said.

"Don't call me Georgie!" he shouted.

"Oh, sorry," Sage said. "I mean you're very funny, *George*."

That was better.

"I've been practicing my twist on the trampoline. Is my acrobat act before or after your clown act?" Sage asked.

George didn't answer. Instead he kept his eyes on the center ring where Julianna was busy taming her animals. Chris the tiger had jumped through a hoop. Then he pretended to go wild, running around seats and roaring. Some of the little kids shrieked, but you could tell they knew it was only pretend.

"Now, ladies and gentlemen, the ferocious wild boar will do a somersault," Julianna said.

Alex crouched and tucked his head down. But before he could roll over, there was **a loud, ripping sound**. *R-r-r-ippp*. Alex's costume tore right down the back.

The kids and their parents began to laugh. George began to laugh, too.

R-R-R-IPPPP.

And then, suddenly, he felt something bubbling **wildly** in his stomach.

George's act was next. At first he thought maybe it was just nervous butterflies in his tummy. But then the bubbling got **stronger**.

Oh no! Not the super burp! Not here in the middle of the circus.

George had to stop the bubbles. They **boing-bing-boinged** up to his chest.

They **bing-boing-binged** their way up his throat. And then . . .

George let out the loudest burp anyone had ever heard. It was louder than a tiger's roar! Louder than a wild boar's oink!

And then, George completely lost control. **The burp was in charge.**

George's feet raced over to the snack stand. His hands grabbed a soda bottle and began shaking it up and down. Then George burst into the ring.

"George! Go away!" Julianna shouted.

"Our act's not over."

George's ears didn't listen to Julianna. His fingers started untwisting the cap on the soda bottle . . . **BOOM**! The bubbly soda exploded out of the bottle—and sprayed all over the kids and the parents.

"Hey! What are you doing?" one of the dads shouted.

"George, cut it out!" Julianna ordered.

But the super burp wouldn't be tamed. George kept spraying the soda until the bottle was empty. Then he ran

back to the snack table, and grabbed the Boston cream pie.

"George, no!" Chris shouted out.

George wanted to put the pie down. But his hands wouldn't cooperate.

George's legs started running around the ring. "Get ready to see a **pie fly**!" he shouted out to the crowd.

"Pies can't fly," a little girl shouted back.

"Wanna bet?" George asked. He stopped running. He raised his eyebrows and grinned. Slowly, George drew back

one arm and took aim—right at Julianna.

"George! Don't you dare—," Julianna began.

Too late! The ooey-gooey Boston cream pie was already soaring through the air.

Julianna was quick. She ducked, and the pie flew right over her head—and hit Alex in the face!

The kids in the audience started to laugh **really hard**.

"What was that for?" Alex shouted.
Chocolate goo and whipped cream was
dripping all over him.

George didn't answer.
Instead, he headed for the
small trampoline.

"Georgie!" Sage shouted. "No
fair! That's *my* act."

George scrambled onto the

trampoline and began jumping.

Boing! Boing! Boing! George bounced **higher and higher** on the trampoline.

"Whee! I'm flying," he cried.

Boing! Boing! George wiggled his rear end for the crowd.

"Ha-ha-ha!" The kids were all laughing.

Boing! George bounced up again. But this time it felt like someone snatched him from behind.

George was hanging in midair. His arms waved. His legs kicked wildly.

The kids laughed harder.

George turned to see what had happened. *Oh no!* He was hanging from the branch of a tree—by **his *underwear*!**

And then . . . suddenly . . . *whoosh!* George felt something pop deep in his belly. It felt like the wind had been knocked right out of him. **The super burp was gone.**

"Ow!" George cried out. "I'm stuck! Get me down from here."

"I'll get a ladder," Chris yelled.

Alex was still wiping goo off his face.
"Mmmm . . . I guess the show is over," he told
the crowd.

"A five-minute circus?" one dad said. "I
want my **money back**."

"So do I," a mom said.

"I didn't even get to do my act," Sage
complained.

"Stop groaning!" George said. "*I'm* the
one with **the world's worst wedgie**."

Chris returned with the ladder. Julianna
held it steady at the bottom as Chris climbed
up. He pulled on the branch.

Crack. The branch **broke**. George landed
on the ground—**hard**.

Chris looked at the broken tree branch.
"My parents aren't going to be happy when
they see this," Chris said.

George wasn't happy, either. He was pretty
sure he had a splinter in his backside.

Stupid super burp. It had ruined
everything . . . again.

Chapter 8

On Monday, the first thing Louie said to George was, "I heard about your circus. You really *cracked* people up."

George didn't say anything.

Max and Mike both said, "Good one, Louie."

"Why would you have a circus, anyway?" Louie said. "Circuses are for **babies**."

"Because we want to buy . . . ," Chris started.

George nudged him in the side before he could finish the sentence. He didn't want Louie to know they were saving up for a remote-controlled Dude-on-a-Skateboard. Louie would **never shut up** about getting one first.

"We like being in business," George said.

"So exactly how much have you made?" Louie asked him.

"Uh, the bell's about to ring," Alex said.

"Right behind you," George said.

"Behind . . ." Louie laughed **in a mean way**. "Good one, George."

"Mrs. Kelly, are you okay?" Sage asked.

Mrs. Kelly had red scratches on her arms, and a long scratch on her cheek.

"My sweet kitty cat, Fester, got upset," Mrs. Kelly said.

"It looks like she got attacked by a boar," Alex whispered to George. "And not the pink piggy kind of boar. **The wild kind**."

The old George would have laughed at that. But George was still trying to be the new, improved George.

"It wasn't actually Fester's fault," Mrs. Kelly explained. "I was cat-sitting for a friend and Fester isn't used to having another kitty in the house. They got into a fight and I got caught in the middle. But I'd never let **my little kitty witty** get hurt."

George choked back another laugh.

"I love all kinds of cats. Fester's a Manx cat. But Siamese cats are beautiful, too," Mrs. Kelly said.

"My family went to Africa on a safari," Louie told Mrs. Kelly. "We saw tigers. Even **a white tiger**."

George rolled his eyes. Louie was always showing off.

"Are we going to study cats?" Sage asked.

"No," Mrs. Kelly told Sage. "We're just having a conversation about pets and the way people love them. After gym class, we'll go back to our unit on Alaska and the Arctic."

"We have gym first this morning?" Alex asked.

Mrs. Kelly nodded. "Except Mr. Trainer isn't here, so I'm your gym teacher today."

George frowned. How come Mr. Trainer was absent so much?

"In fact . . ." Mrs. Kelly's voice drifted off while **a huge, gummy smile** formed on her face.

George gulped. He knew that smile. It was the smile Mrs. Kelly got just before she made the class do something **awful**.

"Do you all know the alley cat dance?" Mrs. Kelly asked the class when they arrived at the gym.

"I don't," Louie said.

"Me neither," Julianna added.

"Well, I'll teach it to you right now," Mrs. Kelly said. "Just do what I do."

341

Mrs. Kelly took dancing **very seriously**. The only way you could get out of one of her dances would be if you had a broken leg. And then she might still make you dance—on your crutches.

Mrs. Kelly put her hands up in front, like cat paws. Then she started to dance. "Right foot. Right foot. Left foot. Left," she sang as she danced. "Right knee.

Right knee. Left knee. Left. And clap and turn."

George frowned. Then it hit him. Something Mrs. Kelly had said was really interesting. Not the right foot, left foot stuff. The thing about people really loving pets. A **big smile** formed on George's face. He knew the perfect business to go into. **This one couldn't miss.**

Chapter 9

"As soon as these hamsters start having babies, we'll make a fortune," George told Chris and Alex. It was Saturday. The boys were in the shed behind George's house.

"I don't know," Chris said. "So far all we've done is **lose** money."

"**Remember what Mrs. Kelly said** about people loving their pets?" George asked. "Who wouldn't love to bring home a cute baby hamster? And we'll have a big supply soon. Hamsters can have as many as seven babies at one time. I read that on a hamster website."

"Maybe that's why Mr. Furstman gave us such a good deal on these hamsters," Alex said.

"Mr. Furstman is a nice guy," George said. Mr. Furstman had also loaned George a big hamster cage. "I know him because his pet shop is in the same shopping center as my mom's store."

"We have two boy hamsters and two girl hamsters," Chris said. "If the girls both have seven babies . . ."

"We'll have **fourteen new hamsters**," Alex said. "And if we sell them at two dollars a piece, we'll

have enough money to buy
the Dude, and earn back
everything we paid
for the food and
stuff."

"Is your
mom okay with us
keeping the hamsters
in here?" Chris asked.

Actually, George had **no idea** if his
mom was okay with it, mostly because
he hadn't asked her. He wasn't exactly
trying to hide the hamsters from his
mom. That was something the old George
would do. *This* George was trying to be
responsible. If the hamsters kept having
babies, before long, George would be able
to pay his mom back for
the ruined material and
broken beads at the

Knit Wit. Paying his mom back would show **maturity**. His mom loved stuff like that, **even more than his special face**.

Besides, George figured his parents wouldn't ever find out about the hamsters. Neither of them ever came into the shed. It was filled with boxes of things from their old house in Cherrydale.

"We have to make sure the cage is kept clean. And they need a lot of water," George told Alex and Chris. "And chew sticks. **Hamsters love chew sticks**."

"You know a lot about hamsters," Chris said.

"Our third-grade class pet at my old school was a hamster," George told him.

George picked

up one of the hamsters and pet it gently on the back. All four of its feet were white. It looked like it was wearing socks.

"At first I was creeped out by Speedy," George said. "Especially when he escaped and wound up in my sneaker. But I got to like him. In fact, this one kind of looks like Speedy. I'm naming it **Speedy 2**."

George stuck an extra chew stick into Speedy 2's cage. "Don't worry," he told the hamster. "I'll come back later and visit."

George did come back. In fact, over the next few days, George spent a lot of his free time in the shed behind his house. He loved being with the hamsters. And lucky for him, the super burp left him alone while he was there. When George was with the hamsters, there wasn't even one mini-bubble in his belly.

Alex and Chris helped out, too. One afternoon when George had to go to the dentist, Alex fed all the hamsters. The next morning, Chris came over and fed them before picking up George for school.

"Speedy 2 is getting **really fat**," Chris said as the boys walked toward school. "Do you think she's a girl hamster and she's going to have babies soon?"

George shrugged. "Maybe. Or it could be that I give her extra treats."

"You shouldn't have favorites, George," Chris said. "We have to like all the hamsters the same."

"I know," George agreed. But **he couldn't help himself**. Speedy 2 was his favorite. It would be kind of cool if she really was getting

ready to have babies. Then there would
be **Speedys 3, 4, 5, 6, 7, 8, and 9**!

George ran home from school to see
if Chris had been right about Speedy 2
being ready to be a mom.

When George got to the shed, there
was a surprise waiting for him. **But it
wasn't a hamster mom.** It was a human
mom. *George's* mom.

"George, do you know
why these **rats** are in my
shed?" his mom asked
angrily, pointing to the
hamster cage.

"They're not rats,

Mom. They're hamsters," George told her.

"I don't care what they are," his mom said. "I want to know why they're here."

"They're going to have babies," he said. "And then Alex, Chris, and I are going to sell them. We're in the **hamster business**."

"You *were* in the hamster business," George's mom said. "Now you're out of it."

"Why?" George asked her.

"Because one of your pets escaped," his mother explained. "It chewed a hole in one of the boxes."

"Hamsters love to chew," George said.

"I figured that out," George's mother told him. "The hamster chewed a hole in a sweater I knitted this summer. His mom held up a blue sweater with a big hole in the front.

Oh man. **This was *ba-a-ad*.** But the sweater hole wasn't the worst of it. When George turned to look at the cage, he realized something awful. The missing hamster was Speedy 2. Chris must not have closed her cage door all the way when he cleaned it that morning.

"Poor Speedy 2," George said. "I have to find her!"

"Yes, you do," his mom agreed.

George got a really worried look on his face. Speedy 2 was **so small**. She could have slipped out from under the door or through a hole in the shed. It was a big world out there. She could be lost . . . **or worse**.

"It's all my fault!" George said. "I can't do anything right."

George's mom took a deep breath. "Look, George, I'm really proud that you tried to start your own business. But animals are a big responsibility. And you should have asked permission."

"I know," George said. "I'm really sorry."

"Once you find the missing hamster," his mother said, "take them all back to the pet shop."

George looked under boxes and in between cartons. He looked on the top shelves. And on the bottom shelves. And then . . . *whish!* Something **small and furry** zoomed across the floor toward the corner of the shed.

George scooped Speedy 2 up in his hands. **Her little hamster heart was beating really fast.**

"Boy, am I going to miss you," he told the hamster.

Chapter 10

"Wow! Mr. Furstman gave us all our money back," Chris said.

"So how come you look so bummed?" Alex asked. "Is it about the RC Dude-on-a-Skateboard?"

"Nah," he said. **"I miss Speedy 2."**

"Can you visit her?" Chris asked him.

"Yeah," George said. "Mr. Furstman said I can stop by the pet shop any time."

"Let's go after school," Chris suggested. "I have to go to the stationery store across the street to get a new blank book. I'm starting another comic book. It's called *Toiletman: Escape from Under the Lid*."

"Aroo! Ruff! Ruff!"

"Tweet! Tweet!"

"Meow!"

Things were really crazy in Mr. Furstman's  pet shop when George got there. Poor Mr. Furstman could **barely keep up**. At the moment, he was busy trying to catch a goldfish and put it in a bag of water for a little girl.

"I want the one that's really **golden**," George heard the little girl tell her mother and Mr. Furstman.

All goldfish looked the same to George. But not to the little girl. When Mr. Furstman handed her a bag with a goldfish in it, she started to yell.

"No!" she shouted. "Not him. **I want the golden one!"**

Just then, a man with a small, brown, furry dog walked up behind Mr. Furstman. "Where do you keep the Pupper Supper dog food?" he asked him. "That's the kind Bruiser likes."

"Third aisle, on the left," Mr. Furstman told him.

"I looked there. I didn't see it," the man said.

George looked over at Mr. Furstman. **He seemed really frazzled.**

"Can I help?" George said.

Mr. Furstman looked up from the fish tank and shot George a smile. "Thanks, George," he said.

"No problem," George answered.

George found the dog food for the man and then went to the next aisle, where the hamster cages were. He was looking for Speedy 2 when Mr. Furstman called out, "George, can you show this woman where the chew sticks are?"

"Sure." George waved to the woman. "They're right over here."

When things calmed down, George went back to check on Speedy 2. Mr. Furstman came over.

"I think she's going to have a litter of babies very soon," Mr. Furstman said.

"Wow," George said. "You're so **lucky**, Mr. Furstman. You get to be around animals all the time."

"It's a good job," Mr. Furstman said. "I love animals. And I like people who love animals, too. You were a big help today. Maybe you'd like to help out more often."

"You mean like **a job**?" George asked.

Mr. Furstman nodded. "You could earn a little extra money and . . ."

"Visit Speedy 2!" George finished Mr. Furstman's sentence.

"Exactly," Mr. Furstman said.

Wow. This was perfect. Or at least **it would be** as long as the stupid super burp stayed away.

Chapter 11

"Say hi, Petey. Hi," George told the green parrot who sat in a cage in the middle of the pet store. "Hi."

"Squawk!" Petey answered.

George rolled his eyes. He'd been trying for three weeks to get Petey to say "hi." But all he did was squawk.

Still, George wasn't giving up. Petey was his best friend in the whole pet store. Speedy 2 had already had her babies, and she was back in a cage with other hamsters. One of her babies had white socks, too.

But Petey was the only parrot in the pet shop, and **he loved George**—especially when George let him ride around on his shoulder. George liked that, too. It made him feel like a **pirate**.

"Say hi," George told Petey again.

"Squawk," Petey answered.

Just then, bells began to ring. That meant someone was coming in. George looked up. It was Alex and Chris.

"Yo, dudes!" George shouted out.

"We came to visit the hamsters," Chris said.

"George, can you feed the garter snakes?" Mr. Furstman called.

"Sure thing, Mr. Furstman." George turned to his friends. "I gotta work."

"Can we watch you feed the snakes?" Alex asked.

"Sure," George said. "But I'm warning you—**it's not pretty**."

George walked over to where Mr. Furstman kept the snake food. Some kids might be freaked out by having to stick their hands into a vat of **wiggly, jiggly** worms.

But not George. Worms were what garter snakes ate.

"Yuck," Chris said. "Aren't they slimy?"

"*Super* slimy," George said. "And they smell, too."

"Wow," Alex said. **"That's so cool."**

George proudly carried a handful of wiggly, jiggly, slimy worms over to the snake cages. **"Dinner time!"** he called out.

Just then a woman carrying a little, white dog walked up behind George. "Young man," she asked. "Do you sell **gourmet** dog food?"

George turned around. The dog was wearing a jeweled collar. The woman was wearing a jeweled necklace. They matched—in a weird **dog, dog-owner** kind of way.

"We sell dog food," George said. "I don't know if it's gourmet."

George was about to say he'd ask

Mr. Furstman, when suddenly something bubbly began wiggling around in his belly. Kind of like a worm.

George hadn't burped once during the three weeks he'd been working at the pet shop. And he wasn't about to let it happen now. He shut his lips tight.

But the burp was **strong**. It had already bounced its way out of his belly and into his chest. Now it was heading straight for his mouth.

"Burp . . ." A tiny little burp slipped out from between George's clenched lips. It wasn't a **supersonic mega burp**, but it was a magic burp. And now it was out there.

"Young man!" the woman scolded. "That's disgusting. You should say '**excuse me**.'"

George knew that was true. But he also knew he couldn't say that—or anything else. He was afraid to open his mouth. A bigger burp might slip out.

"Now where is the dog food?" the woman said.

George reached out his hand and pointed to the dog food aisle.

"Aaah!" the rich woman shouted. She almost dropped her dog.

George looked at his hand. *Uh-oh.* He'd just pointed to the dog food with some worms dangling from his fingers.

"Get those things out of my sight!" the woman told George.

That was all it took. **The burp could no longer be controlled.** It just had to do something funny. George's mouth popped open. And his hand dropped the worms right down his throat.

The worms wiggled inside his mouth.
Gulp. George's throat swallowed hard.
Down went the wiggling, jiggling worms
right into George's belly.

The woman looked like she was going
to faint.

"Whoa!" Chris shouted. "Dude! I can't
believe you did that!"

"Awesome!" Alex added.
He sounded seriously
impressed.

Whoosh. Just
then George felt
something go pop
deep inside. Sort
of like a needle
bursting a
balloon. It was
like the air went
rushing out of
him.

Unfortunately, the customer rushed out, too. "I'll never come back here again," she said in a loud voice—loud enough for Mr. Furstman to hear.

"George!" Mr. Furstman shouted as he ran across the store.

Uh-oh. Was George about to lose another job?

"You guys better get out of here," George told Alex and Chris. "Go look at the hamsters or something."

Alex and Chris nodded. They hurried away before Mr. Furstman got to where George was standing.

"Are you okay?" Mr. Furstman asked George.

Huh? George was pretty confused. **He was fine.**

"That dog bit me once," Mr. Furstman told him. "So when I see him, I get nervous."

George shook his head. "Nah. He didn't bite me. But his owner said she wasn't ever coming back here."

"That's fine with me," Mr. Furstman told George. "She never buys anything, anyway. She just complains that we don't sell anything fancy enough for her **precious pooch**."

George laughed. The way Mr. Furstman had said "precious pooch" sounded just like the lady.

"You okay to go restock the kitty litter shelves?" Mr. Furstman asked George.

"Sure thing!" George said happily.

As he walked off to get the kitty litter, George smiled. He still had a job.

Take that, super burp!

Chapter 12

"Hi, Mr. Tyler," George said as he, Alex, Chris, and Julianna walked into the toy store on Sunday morning. "We're here to buy the remote-controlled Dude-on-a-Skateboard."

"I still can't believe we **really have all the money we need**," Alex whispered excitedly.

George nodded. "And a couple of dollars left over for extra batteries."

"Awesome!" Chris and Julianna said.

Mr. Tyler looked at the kids and shook his head. **"I'm sorry,"** he said, "but I sold the last one yesterday."

"No way," Alex said.

"You gotta be kidding," Chris added.

George didn't say anything. He couldn't. He was too bummed to talk.

"But I have some other cool toys," Mr. Tyler said. "How about a really amazing **chemistry set**?"

George shook his head. "I don't think my parents would want me to get anything where I could blow up stuff."

"Me neither," Chris agreed.

"The only thing we really wanted was the Dude-on-a-Skateboard," Julianna said.

"I'm sorry," Mr. Tyler said. "I guess you should have come in sooner."

"We didn't have the money sooner," Alex said.

George looked at the floor. He **knew it was his fault** they hadn't gotten the money in time. Well, not his fault, really. **The super burp's fault.**

George and his pals were not in very good moods when they left the toy store. As they passed by the park, they spotted Louie, Max, and Mike. Louie was kicking and stomping something on the ground.

"I wonder what that's all about," Julianna said.

"Let's go see," George said. He and his friends turned and walked into the park.

"Hey, Louie, what's up?" George asked.

"He's **mad**," Mike said.

"*Real* mad," Max added.

"At what?" George asked.

"At this stupid Dude-on-a-Skateboard," Louie grumbled. "What a hunk of junk."

"It's junk," Max agreed.

"A whole hunk," Mike added.

"What happened to it?" Alex asked.

"It popped a wheel," Louie said.

"You mean **it popped a *wheelie***," George corrected him.

Louie shook his head. "No. I mean it popped a wheel. The back wheel fell off. And then the dude's arm broke in half. **Stupid toy!**"

"Wow, that's too bad," George said.

"It's gonna be too bad for that toy store!" Louis shouted. "If they don't give me my money back, my dad's gonna sue them. **He's a big-time lawyer, you know.**"

George *didn't* know that. And he had never heard of anyone suing a toy store over a fifteen dollar toy, either. But he *was* glad he'd found out **the Dude-on-a-Skateboard toy wasn't so great**, after all.

He turned to his friends. "We gotta get going, right, guys?"

Julianna, Alex, and Chris nodded.

As they walked away, Alex said, "Boy, that was close."

"I know," Chris said.

"I can't believe we almost wasted fifteen dollars on a remote-controlled **hunk of junk**," George said.

"I guess we were lucky it took us so long to get the money," Julianna said.

George smiled. He knew luck had

nothing to do with it. The super burp was what had kept them from getting the money fast enough.

Amazing. George was **actually glad** about something the super burp had done. But just this once.

About the Author

Nancy Krulik is the author of more than 150 books for children and young adults including three *New York Times* best sellers and the popular Katie Kazoo, Switcheroo books. She lives in New York City with her family, and many of George Brown's escapades are based on things her own kids have done. (No one delivers a good burp quite like Nancy's son, Ian!) Nancy's favorite thing to do is laugh, which comes in pretty handy when you're trying to write funny books!

About the Illustrator

Aaron Blecha was raised by a school of giant squid in Wisconsin and now lives with his family by the English seaside. He works as an artist designing toys, animating cartoons, and illustrating books, including the Zombiekins and The Rotten Adventures of Zachary Ruthless series. You can enjoy more of his weird creations at www.monstersquid.com.

George Brown, CLASS CLOWN

**Read all the books in the
GEORGE BROWN, CLASS CLOWN series!**